THE KING'S SHILLING

OTHER BOOKS BY
DAVID STARR

The Nor'Wester (2017)

Golden Game (2017)

Golden Goal (2017)

From Bombs to Books (2011)

THE
KING'S SHILLING

David Starr

RONSDALE PRESS

THE KING'S SHILLING
Copyright © 2018 David Starr

RONSDALE PRESS
3350 West 21st Avenue, Vancouver, B.C., Canada V6S 1G7
www.ronsdalepress.com

Typesetting: Julie Cochrane, in Minion 12 pt on 16
Cover Art & Design: Nancy de Brouwer, Massive Graphic Design
Paper: 55 lb. Enviro Book Antique Natural (FSC) 100% post-consumer
     waste, totally chlorine-free and acid-free

Ronsdale Press wishes to thank the following for their support of its publishing program: the Canada Council for the Arts, the Government of Canada, the British Columbia Arts Council, and the Province of British Columbia through the British Columbia Book Publishing Tax Credit program.

 Canada Council   Conseil des arts
for the Arts   du Canada

 BRITISH COLUMBIA
ARTS COUNCIL
An agency of the Province of British Columbia

Library and Archives Canada Cataloguing in Publication

Starr, David, author
   The king's shilling / David Starr. — First edition.

Issued in print and electronic formats.
ISBN 978-1-55380-526-7 (softcover)
ISBN 978-1-55380-527-4 (ebook) / ISBN 978-1-55380-528-1 (pdf)

   I. Title.

PS8637.T365K56 2018   jC813'.6   C2018-900532-7   C2018-900533-5

At Ronsdale Press we are committed to protecting the environment. To this end we are working with Canopy and printers to phase out our use of paper produced from ancient forests. This book is one step towards that goal.

Printed in Canada by Marquis Printing, Quebec

for Sherry

ACKNOWLEDGEMENTS

I would like to thank my parents Ken and Yvonne Starr for their support and love throughout the years. I would also like to acknowledge all members of my family, past and present, who served in the armed forces of the United Kingdom, especially those who gave their lives in defence of their country. Finally, I would like to thank Ron and Veronica Hatch for their continued support of Canadian writers telling stories that matter to Canadian readers.

Chapter 1

THE SCENT OF CREOSOTE, salt water and sewage fills the Merseyside air as I disembark from the *Caroline*.

We sailed from Quebec City four weeks ago, the crossing uneventful. We avoided icebergs, storms, French warships and any number of other hazards that plague travel on the Atlantic, and as we dock I say a grateful farewell to the captain who brought me home safe and in one piece.

I climb down the gangway onto the wooden decking of the Liverpool dock then pause for a minute, remembering bitterly the last time I stood here.

Not two slips down from this very spot, my sister Libby

sacrificed her freedom to save me, at a price I can only guess as I hid on board the migrant ship the *Sylph*, sailing away to Canada while Libby was taken away by red-coated soldiers. I owe her my life. I must find her.

I pick up my bag and walk. I know where I'm going, have been here before, and when I round a corner to see the same warehouse where Tinker, the man whom we trusted, betrayed us, my heart races.

I scan the waterfront, half expecting to find the treacherous little man and his pony cart, but there is no sight of him. A fortunate thing for Tinker. Goodness knows what I would do if I ever saw the villain again.

I compose myself and am about to head into the city and begin my search when I'm stopped by an old woman standing against a post. "Spare a penny, Sir?" she asks politely, holding out a small tin cup.

"Aye, of course," I say, depositing a coin into her cup. Between my wages from my three years in the wilds of North America and the leftover coins from my passage back to Liverpool, paid by the North West Company, I can easily afford a copper or two.

"Thank you, Sir," she says, flashing a toothless smile as she ambles off down the dock.

"I'm glad to see you've learned a little something about charity since the last time I saw you, lad," says an unexpected voice from behind. I turn quickly to see the same legless sailor I'd met the day I left Liverpool, leaning against a crate.

I hadn't thought of him for years, but I recognize him at once.

John his name was, an old sailor who lost his legs fighting the Spanish at Cape St. Vincent with Admiral Nelson. He was there, on that day we were betrayed by Tinker, the day I escaped and Libby was captured by the soldiers.

John shuffles towards me, inching his legless frame along. "You're older now and with that goose down on your chin you could almost pass for a man. The lass you were with gave me money. You weren't happy about it, from what I recall."

"Aye, that was my sister. I'm trying to find her. The soldiers took her away."

"They did at that," he says. "You caused quite the commotion that day, you pair. I must say I'm surprised to see you again, lad. I heard you were lost at sea, went down to Davy Jones' locker. That's what the papers said anyway."

"Papers? What are ye talking about?" I try to suppress my panic. I've not been back in England twenty minutes and already here is someone who knows I'm alive.

"Don't you worry about old John," the sailor says, as if he can read my mind. "The Old Bailey pronounced you dead at her trial, so far be it from me to contradict the courts. Let the dead stay dead, that's what I say. I won't be telling the authorities you've come back from the grave."

"Trial? What trial?" I demand. First he speaks of papers and now a trial. "Do ye ken what happened to Libby? Please, tell me."

"Do I know what happened?" he chortles. "The entire country knows what happened. All the newspapers in England wrote about your sister, told her story to every man, woman and child in the kingdom, they did!"

"What do ye mean *her story*?" I grab the man by the shoulders, my heart filled with a desperate hope this man knows where I can find my sister.

"Easy, lad!" the crippled sailor protests. "I ain't the one who took her!"

I let him go. "I'm sorry," I say, struggling to control my emotions. "Please, tell me if ye ken where Libby is."

"What's it worth to you? You was most kind to that old lady; I wouldn't mind seeing your new-found generosity once more."

I quickly give the man a small silver coin. "Tell me all ye ken and ye'll have another."

John eagerly takes the money. "'Twas a most remarkable thing," he begins. "What a brave little lassie she is! Like I said, newspapers across the land told her tale. I can't read meself of course, but one or two of the brighter lads here can. We all followed her adventures, down on the waterfront. Even tried to help her escape I did, after she was taken by the soldiers. A right good little trick; you hiding on that old coal boat and her sending the hounds after the wrong fox as it were."

I remember it well. When I was hidden on the *Sylph* I could hear the redcoats taking Libby away, heard her say I had sailed on another ship. The *Leopard* it was called, a ship destined to hit an iceberg off Newfoundland and sink with all hands.

"Aye, boy, your sister's plight was even talked about in the House of Commons!" John says. His voice drops to a whisper, as if he is about to tell me some great secret. "Some even say she talked to the prime minister himself, but who's to say if that ain't just a fairy tale?"

"Please," I beg, "fairy story or no tell me everything ye can. I'm desperate fer news."

For the next ten minutes or so the old sailor relates to me all that he knows. If only half of it is true, the most awful, remarkable things have happened to my sister.

"She was supposed to swing from the gibbet at Newgate Prison," John says, my heart nearly beating out of my chest as I listen. "That was her sentence after all, for helping you skip the country, but then that woman stepped in."

"Woman? What woman?" I demand.

"Elizabeth Fry, one of them famous Quaker do-gooders who helps the convicts. She's the one who took your sister's story to the newspapers. Saved her life she did, managed to get her sentence changed to transportation."

"Transportation? To where?" The crippled sailor can't speak quickly enough for me.

"Oh lad," John says. "Your sister was to be shipped off to Australia with all the other convicts."

"Australia? She went to Australia?" I can't imagine that

Libby is gone, shipped to the very bottom of the world just as I finally reach home.

"Well that's the thing of it, ain't it?" he tells me. "It was round about then your sister disappeared. Vanished, she did, into thin air."

I give the sailor two more coins. "Is there anything else ye ken? I need to find her! Tell me, quickly!"

"Sorry, lad, that's all I know," says John, though he still pockets my coins, "so if I were you I'd go to London and find Elizabeth Fry. She knew your sister best. She may even know where she is — if she's even still alive."

Chapter 2

IT IS ONE SMALL piece of luck that Elizabeth Fry is in London. After all, I have pledged to carry one more letter for the North West Company, and that message must be delivered to the capital.

For a handful of shillings I buy passage on the mail coach from Liverpool to London. It is a considerable amount of money, and at first I contemplate walking, or perhaps even buying my own horse and riding there, but the crippled sailor advised against both before I bid him farewell.

"'Tis a dangerous journey to London by yourself," John had told me. "Brigands and highwaymen are everywhere. They'd slit your throat for the gold in your purse, or even the hope of it. Travelling in the safety of numbers is a far better idea."

It isn't that I'm afraid of bandits. After crossing North America from Quebec to the Pacific Ocean and back, I've come to know danger and how to take care of myself. Rather, my concern is the time it would take me to get to London. To walk the nearly two hundred miles would consume the better part of a week, and that is time I desperately need.

Travelling alone on horseback holds little appeal either, if truth be told. In New Caledonia I spent some time with horses along Fraser's River when the water was too turbulent to paddle. I rode across the grasslands at Red River as well, I remember sadly, with the Métis girl Louise Desjarlais and her massive black horse, Kavalé. It has been more than two years since she died, but Louise's memory is still a raw sore in my heart.

Cost or not, the mail coach is my best option. There's a daily service between Liverpool and London, and the coach has room for passengers as well as the post. It has fast become a popular means of travel and I secure the last seat on board.

The mail coach leaves at sunrise so I rent a room in a small inn off the waterfront for the night. After nearly two months at sea I'm desperate for a good meal, and so I treat myself to roast lamb and a glass of ale as well. A man can eat dry pork and biscuits for only so long, and the thought of warm bread, fresh meat and a cool drink makes my mouth water.

The innkeeper delivers my food and I eat alone, deep in thought by a large fireplace that crackles merrily as I sip slowly on my beer. I've not developed a taste for the rum favoured by the Nor'Westers back in North America, nor for the gin consumed in vast amounts by the poor of England. Beer is palatable, however, and far safer than drinking water straight from the River Mersey.

I retire to my room before the sun goes down. I'm tired but there's work to do before I sleep, work I need to do in private without any prying eyes. Once I'm in my room and the door is safely locked behind me, I take out my knife, a gift from my friend Tom on the *Sylph*.

The edge is as sharp as a razor. It has seen its share of blood as well, most noticeably that of the Nor'Wester La Malice, dead at my hands on the bank of Fraser's River after he tried to murder Simon Fraser, the leader of our expedition. And me.

I put the knife to a less deadly use right now, slicing open the lining of my cloak and the waistband of my trousers. I need to safeguard my money, my wages for three years in the wilderness, as well as the bonus paid me by Mr. McGillivray for delivering the confidential message I am carrying to the War Office in London.

I feel inside the deep pocket of my cloak for a small oilskin pouch. Within that pouch is a sealed secret letter for the secretary of state for the colonies himself, and for no other. It is not the message McGillivray had wanted to write, however.

The leader of the North West Company's dearest hope had been to let the Empire know that the Columbia River was in British hands and the Nor'Westers had found a navigable route to the Pacific.

Instead, McGillivray must inform London that the river we travelled was not the Columbia, but another one now named after Simon Fraser, its currents far too dangerous for any commercial undertakings.

I leave a few coins in my pocket for expenses over the next week or so, tuck the rest into the lining of my clothes then sew up the slits. My money is safer hidden within my clothes than in a bag in my pocket, easily stolen by highwaymen or lost on a bumpy road.

I haven't slept on firm ground since leaving Quebec, and as I lie in my bed, tucked in under a warm blanket, it is difficult at first to fall asleep without the rocking of the boat on the waves beneath me.

Soon my eyes grow heavy, however, and I start to drift off. Before I fall asleep, I think of my sister. Libby is out there somewhere, and I won't stop looking until I find her. Libby saved my life, the debt I owe her long overdue.

Chapter 3

I RISE BEFORE THE sun, eat a slice of bread and a piece of
cold lamb left over from supper then pack my few belong-
ings into my bag and make my way to the mail coach. "Welcome, boyo," says the driver as I give him my ticket. "You can
ride inside or outside beside me. It's all the same to me."

"Beside ye if I may. I'd prefer the fresh air."

"Then climb up and take your seat," he says. "We leave in
ten minutes, and up here you'll have all the fresh air you
need."

The man who will take me to London is a small Welshman named Evans, with black curly hair and a musical lilt in
his voice. I do as he says, greeting the four passengers who

travel inside, two older couples by the looks of things, men and women who seem indifferent to me at best.

"Right then," Evans says. "Time to go." He clicks his tongue, snaps the reins and the coach moves forward with a jolt as the eager horses pull away. "Within two days we'll be in London and with that bloke along, the highwaymen won't bother us," Evans tells me as we canter through the streets of Liverpool.

The *him* the coach driver refers to is the last person on the coach I see, a man in a scarlet-and-gold uniform who sits alone in the seat behind me, a dangerous-looking blunderbuss in his arms, a brace of pistols in his belt. "Royal Mail guard," the coachman explains, "sworn to keep the post safe. Good at his job but not much of a conversationalist, are you, Fred?"

"I let this do the talking, Evans," the guard says curtly in response, looking at his blunderbuss.

It is a nasty piece of business, the blunderbuss, able to fire a load of shot or a large lead ball. It is a smaller, hand-held version of the swivel gun Simon Fraser took with us on our trip down his river but just as lethal at close quarters.

Evans grins. "A full sentence! He's chatty today, our Fred. I've made the trip to London and back with Fred here two dozen times and I can count the number of words he's said to me on one hand."

"Guid morning," I say to the guard, though I am not as fortunate enough as Evans to get a reply. Instead the man gives me a suspicious look and a cursory tip of his head.

Nobody sits by the Royal Mail guard. He doesn't talk much to Evans either, just sits there on his seat, eyes scanning the road ahead as we leave Liverpool, the coach and leather harnesses creaking, traces jingling as we move.

"Tough bugger, that Freddy. All the Royal Mail guards are. No matter what the danger or the weather they stay in their perch, the mail locked in the trunk at their feet all safe like. They won't go inside even when the snow comes and they get covered in it. You wouldn't believe what some winters are like on the mail coach."

"I do have some experience with winter," I tell Evans, remembering the blizzard that trapped Luc Lapointe and me under our canoe on the shores of Lake Superior, on our long voyage back to Montreal from Fort St. James.

"Canada, you say? Then I'd wager you're a tough bugger as well. The winters there are cold enough to freeze a man solid from what I hear."

"Aye. I spent the better part of the last three years in the wilds. The snow and ice out there are something to behold." Although the mail coach fairly flies above its hard-packed surface as we chat, I still find it impossible to believe the driver, who assures me again that we will travel the two hundred miles in less than two days.

"In Canada there were times when we considered ten miles in one day a guid distance," I tell him, "and that was with heavy packs on our backs and our canoes over our heads."

"Twenty years ago a coach would have been lucky to make

ten miles in a day as well," Evans tells me, "but thanks to the turnpikes, we fairly fly through the countryside now."

The turnpikes are indeed remarkable. Hundreds of miles of these new roads spread across England now, from the Scottish border to the far southwest. They are not cheap, however.

Our fare to ride on the coach includes our share of the tolls, money Evans gives to the men stationed at the toll-houses we encounter on the road south.

It is a great deal of money, no doubt, but the convenience and the time saved is well worth the cost. Soon I will be in London where I will complete my last duty for the North West Company and begin my search for Libby.

The day is overcast and grey, and though the skies threaten rain, it holds off as the horses trot steadily along the turn-pike to London. Evans stops every two hours or so at post offices along the way, with the Royal Mail guard handing out or taking on letters and other small packages from the post-master. At these stops, the horses are changed out while the passengers are given a chance to stretch their legs.

"How are ye enjoying the ride?" I ask one of the passengers on our first break, one of the two older men, well-dressed with a bushy moustache. I am sharing the road with these people for two days after all, and it is only right I should make conversation with them.

"Fine, thank you," he says curtly, before taking his wife's hand and walks away.

"Don't worry about that lot," says Evans. "Figure themselves lords and ladies of the manor, too good to chat with the likes of us. Me though, I like a good story, so feel free to tell me all about your adventures in Canada."

With fresh horses in the trappings we continue our journey. Time passes quickly by as Evans and I talk. I tell him all about life in Canada, travelling the rivers, my encounters with the people who live there. In turn, Evans speaks of life in the valleys of South Wales, of the small mining town of Caerphilly, where he was born.

It is nearly dusk when the silhouette of a lone rider appears on the side of the road in front of us. "Company ahead, Fred," says Evans, ending the conversation abruptly. "Do you see?"

The Royal Mail guardsman has seen the horseman as well. He sets his pistols on the seat beside him, then takes the short-barrelled blunderbuss into his hands.

"Steady, Evans," the guard says. "Nice and steady." The horses slow down to a trot as we approach. Evans leans down and opens up a small chest in front of him. Two pistols are within.

"What's going on?" I ask.

"I ain't sayin' for certain that fellow ahead fancies himself Dick Turpin," the driver says, reaching inside the chest for one of the pistols, "but lone riders in long black cloaks waiting on the side of the turnpike generally ain't farmers or innkeepers."

A highwayman. It has to be. "I can fire a pistol," I tell Evans, my breath quickening. "I learned to shoot in Canada."

"Fred, what do you think?" Evans asks the guard. "Might be good to have another hand."

"Couldn't hurt," the guard says, as he cocks back the hammer of the blunderbuss. "Three guns to one will make him think twice."

"Go ahead then, boyo," Evans says. "Don't point the thing at him unless Freddy gives you the word but have it nice and visible."

"Keep the doors shut and your mouths shut, all you inside the coach," says Evans to the passengers below us. "We've got a bit of company out here and I don't think they want to ask us if we know the way to Stoke."

The distance between the rider and the mail coach evaporates. Soon we pull even with him. The man is dressed all in black. A long black cloak, black shirt, breeches and a large black hat. I am surprised to see he's not much older than I am.

"Good evening to you, stranger," says Evans, his voice calm and polite. I keep my eyes on the rider, watching him intently. At his waist I see a sword on his left side, the handle of a pistol on his right.

"Good evening, back," the rider says, though he speaks to the guard instead of the driver. To anyone riding past, it would seem as if two acquaintances have stopped to greet each other, but I can feel the tension, can almost read the rider's mind as he takes the measure of Fred — and of us.

The rider's eyes travel from the flintlock blunderbuss in Fred's hand to the pistols Evans and I hold on our laps. His own hand rests on the pommel of his saddle, within easy reach of either weapon he carries.

His hand moves. I draw a breath and tighten my grip on the pistol. But instead of moving to his waist the rider reaches for his hat, tipping it slightly at us.

"Safe travels, my friends. The road can be a dangerous place."

"And to you," Evans replies with cold courtesy. With a click of his heels the rider spurs his horse on. The animal gallops away to the north, clods of dirt kicked up by his heels.

"We'd have heard 'stand and deliver' and have ended the day short our purses and very likely our lives if we weren't armed, boyo," says Evans. "A highwayman for certain, eh, Fred?"

"No doubt," the guard says. "Well done, lad," he says to me.

"High praise, indeed!" says Evans with a grin. "A 'well done, lad' from our Fred here is worth more than a medal pinned on your chest by the King himself!"

The sun has long disappeared by the time we reach Wolverhampton. "Not quite halfway there," Evans says gratefully as he pulls the horses to a stop beside a coach house called the Lamb and Flag. "Time for a well-earned mug of hot cider and some roast beef, don't you think?"

The other passengers most certainly do. The early spring

night is cool, and rain threatens overhead. They climb down from the coach and head straight into the light and warmth of the inn. I wonder if they know how close they came to being robbed.

"I'll have 'em send a meal and a mug of ale up to your room, Fred," says Evans as the Royal Mail guard unloads the heavy trunk he guards as if it were the Crown Jewels themselves.

"Mr. Evans, I'm guid with horses," I say as Evans starts to loosen the bridles. "Let me help ye take them out of the harnesses and feed them. They worked harder than I did today. They deserve to eat first."

"First pistols now horses! I'll not be chopsing at such a kind offer, boyo," the Welshman says gratefully. "The stables are to the left of the inn. We'll get the horses out of their livery, let 'em have a good drink then we'll rub 'em down and give 'em their hay and oats. When the horses are tended to it will be food and drink for us. We're almost halfway to London, boyo," Evans tells me again. "This time tomorrow you'll be eating your tea in the biggest city on earth!"

Chapter 4

"THANK YE FER THE RIDE," I say to Evans as the coach pulls up at the Royal Mail Headquarters on Lombard Street. Fred, the Royal Mail guard, grunts a goodbye to me as he heads into the large building, trunk in hand.

I climb down from the coach and take in my surroundings. London is truly the most remarkable, busy, dirty place I have ever seen in my entire life. The city is massive, dwarfing Glasgow, Montreal, Liverpool and Quebec City combined, and I am overwhelmed by its sheer size. I have never seen a place like this great city, with its buildings five, six even seven storeys tall.

The air is terrible as well, even worse than Glasgow's, I

think, with the coal smoke from what must be a million chimneys turning the evening sky above me grey.

In the West, the Nor'Westers would go weeks without seeing another person. In London, however, the weight of humanity feels like it will crush the very breath from my chest. Suddenly I long for the quiet and empty space of the plains, the western forest or the sea.

I feel dizzy. My head spins as I stumble a little, stretching out my hand onto the side of the coach to catch my balance.

"Are you all right, boyo?" the coach driver says. I realize that Evans is looking at me, concern on his face. "You've gone a bit pale."

"I'm fine, thank ye," I say, catching my breath. "I just felt a wee bit faint is all." It is the city itself that made me feel this way. Finding Libby will not be an easy task in such a place.

Evans nods in agreement. "London has that effect on people first time they see it. When I first came here from my small valley, I thought I would go mad from all the noise and the people. Even now I don't like staying here more than a day or two. Where in London does your business take you?"

"The Colonial Office," I say. "I have a letter to deliver." I instantly regret that I told Evans anything. The letter I carry bears very important news from Simon Fraser for the Empire itself. I had no business telling the coach driver where I was heading. "It's nothing of any importance, business related."

Evans seems impressed nevertheless. "The Colonial Office? That is indeed an interesting answer. I'd have expected you were looking for a job or an old sweetheart or something like that. Instead, you're a postman, just like Fred and me! You should have said something in Liverpool. I'd have given you a discount on your ticket!"

"Do ye ken where the Colonial Office is?" Since Evans now knows where I'm going, I may as well ask for directions. I have no idea where the place is. I keep my other reason to be in London secret, although I like and trust the man. That part of my journey is not his concern at all.

"Aye, boyo, I do," says Evans. "Not far from here. Two miles at most. Head south to the River Thames, turn right then follow the water. Anyone you meet along the road will tell you the rest of the way from there."

"Thank ye, Mr. Evans," I say.

"Think nothing of it, boyo. Though I dare say it's too late in the day to deliver your message now. Night is falling and the place will be locked up tight. If I were you I'd find myself a little tavern, get a room, have an ale or two and finish up my business in the morning."

The coach driver is right. No doubt the secretary of state for the colonies has long since left his office.

"Do ye happen to ken of any places nearby I could stay?" I ask.

"Walk south. In about ten minutes you'll reach the Thames where you'll see a little place called The Gun. It ain't much to look at but the food is good enough and the rooms clean.

You'll get a good night's sleep and be on your way in the morning. Good luck on your travels, boyo. It was a pleasure meeting you."

"And ye as well. Thank ye fer both yer company and advice," I say, shaking Evans' hand. Farewells made, I take my bag from the coach, sling it over my shoulder and make my way to the river.

* * *

I find the place easily enough. The Gun is full of sailors and dockhands, rough-looking men who would have scared me three years ago, but after all my time with North West Company voyageurs, I can hold my own in their company. I pay for a room, as well as a meal of cold roast pork, then I take a seat at a rough wooden table in the dining room and wait for my food.

When dinner comes I eat it quickly then climb up the stairs to my room, lock the door then throw myself onto the bed. I have just enough energy left to take off my boots before crawling under the blanket, falling deep asleep.

I wake up at dawn, slip my boots back on, make my way down the stairs and leave the inn, following the river west as Evans instructed me.

It is simple enough to find the Colonial Office. I need to ask directions only once as I walk, and not twenty minutes from The Gun I reach a large, columned building that hums with activity, even at this early hour.

Stern-faced politicians in black suits and military officers in brightly coloured uniforms come and go from the whitestone building — on important missions of state, no doubt.

William McGillivray, the head of the North West Company, knew I was a wanted fugitive in England and gave me identification papers in the name of McTavish.

I nervously introduce myself as such to an armed soldier at the main gates of the building. I state that I am an envoy from North America with an important message to be given to the secretary of state for the colonies personally.

I am escorted into the building then wait impatiently inside the front door, guarded by a menacing soldier. A clerk disappears inside, but after thirty minutes or more he doesn't return, and I start to get frustrated. I wish the man would return. I'm desperate to find my sister but I have this one last mission for the North West Company to complete, and for Mr. McGillivray I'll do it, though precious minutes slip away.

"Follow me," the clerk says when he finally returns. He leads me briskly up flights of marble stairs until we reach a large wooden door, guarded by two more red-coated soldiers. The clerk knocks politely and walks away, leaving me alone with the soldiers. A moment later the door swings open and the soldiers step aside, allowing me to enter.

"Come in and be quick about it," beckons a voice from within the room. I enter the spacious office and see, through large windows, the River Thames running placidly below. Large charts hang on the wall. My eyes are drawn to one in particular, a map of North America covered with three coloured lines. I find Montreal then look west, across the prairie to the Rocky Mountains, and the Pacific Ocean beyond.

"You're familiar with that country, I'd wager," says a red-haired man with a faint Irish accent. "I am Viscount Castlereagh, secretary of state for war and the colonies. I understand you have a message for me of great importance from McGillivray of the North West Company. I apologize for the wait, but you can understand I'm a very busy man these days, what with Napoleon trying to destroy the British Empire."

Castlereagh motions for me to sit down in a leather armchair. "What's your name, boy? I like to know who it is I'm talking to."

"McTavish, Sir," I say, handing over the sealed envelope McGillivray gave me back in Montreal.

Castlereagh takes the letter. "You're awfully young to have been given the weighty responsibility of travelling across the ocean with a diplomatic despatch, Mr. McTavish."

Despite the seriousness of the situation, a small smile crosses my lips. "Did I say something funny?" the viscount asks, his eyebrow arching.

"Nae, my laird," I say. "I mean no disrespect, but I'm almost nineteen and the voyage from Montreal was by far the easiest trip I've taken in quite some time."

Castlereagh breaks the seal and starts to read. He is a busy man and however curious this diversion is, I know he has serious business to attend to. England is at war with France, after all. Castlereagh quickly scans through the pages, then places the letter on his desk.

"My predecessor, William Windham, and his preoccupation with the Pacific, would have found this all very interesting," says the viscount, "but he is gone and Europe is burning. Napoleon is on the march, country after country is falling to his guns. News about the North West Company's financial difficulties and a river in some god-forsaken corner of North America are of little concern to the Empire these days. They will be addressed when the war with France ends. If it ever does. Thank you for your service, Mr. McTavish," says Castlereagh. "You may go."

There is no mistaking the tone. The most remarkable journey of my life means nothing to him. I am free to leave, my duty to both the North West Company and the British Empire complete.

Chapter 5

IT IS TIME TO FIND Elizabeth Fry. She is the only person on earth who may know where Libby may be. Back in Liverpool, Old John said she was famous, but in the vastness of London the thought of finding one person, no matter how well known, seems almost impossible, a task made harder when I start to ask after Fry.

Famous or not, at first nobody has a clue who I'm talking about. I ask person after person over the next half an hour, and I start to panic until I chance upon an older woman selling apples in a market stall.

"Of course I know who Elizabeth Fry is," she says. "She's a saint, she is. Them prisons are terrible places. Newgate 'specially. What kind of country are we to lock up old women and young girls for years, and for the most minor offences? She's got the ear of the prime minister they say, and will reform our prison system."

"Horse feathers!" says a man walking past who overhears our conversation. "What do you want with that meddling Quaker busybody? You ain't a con, are you, boy?"

"Nae, Sir," I tell him. "Mrs. Fry has been helping a friend of mine. I came to say thank ye to her."

My answer does not allay the man's ill will towards Mrs. Fry — or to me. "In that case, your friend is a no-good criminal, and that damnable woman has been *helping* him evade justice, no doubt. Good day to you, Sir."

"Never you mind him," the woman says. "I don't know where Mrs. Fry lives exactly, but they say she has a house in Newham. It ain't far from here, actually. Just a short walk from here north up Lombard Street will get you to Newham. I'm sure somebody will point you in the right direction once you get there."

I thank the woman and give her a shilling for her help. This is a fantastic piece of luck and well worth the coin. I find Lombard Street easily enough and walk north, a spring in my step, feeling more hopeful about finally finding my sister than I have in years.

* * *

Within the hour I reach the borough of Newham. This is definitely Elizabeth Fry's neighbourhood. Mrs. Fry is very well known in this part of London, and more than a few know where she lives.

The elegant, three-storey home isn't hard to locate. Fry's home is called Plashet House. I approach the front door, gather my nerves and knock. I don't know what Elizabeth Fry looks like, or how she will react when she sees me, but she is my best hope of finding Libby.

A moment later the door opens. "Yes? What do you want?" It is a maid, a pinch-faced young woman who sneers down her nose at me.

"Guid evening," I say politely. "I'm wondering if I may have a word with Mrs. Fry."

"The missus don't see prisoners at her home, released or otherwise."

"Ye misunderstand," I say. "I'm nae a prisoner nor a criminal."

"Then who are you and what do you want with the missus?" the maid demands, no less contemptuous of me than before.

What do I say? I could tell her I'm Libby Scott's brother, but that would be a most foolhardy thing to do. Duncan Scott is supposed to be dead along with the other poor souls on the *Leopard*. "Mrs. Fry and myself have a mutual acquaintance," I say after racking my brains.

"Well, you're out of luck," the maid says, slightly less suspicious of my intentions. "The missus and her husband are on their way back from Bristol; they've been visiting family there. She'll be back in two days, maybe three. May I have your name so I can tell her you called?"

"John Stuart," I tell her, deciding not to use McTavish but the name of my old travelling companion in New Caledonia. I tip my hat at her and leave. "My thanks to ye," I say. "I'll return in three days."

Chapter 6

I NEED AN INEXPENSIVE place to stay until Elizabeth Fry returns, and The Gun is just the place. It is less than two hours' walk back to The Gun from the Quaker woman's house, so I return to the inn on the banks of the Thames, book a room for three nights and go to the common room for supper.

I feel more comfortable now amongst the crowd who frequent The Gun. Many, I notice, are from all over the world by the looks of them. I must have the look of the traveller about me myself, as I'm not given a second glance by any of them.

"Are you wanting to sign on with a ship, lad?" asks a sailor who comes up to me as I eat. He's a bluff man, bald with skin burned brown as a nut by salt and tropical sun. "You know your way around a ship, I wager. I can tell a mariner when I see one."

"Aye. I sailed with Captain Smith on the *Sylph*, a migrant ship out of Liverpool." It isn't a lie, exactly. Mostly I worked in the galley alongside Francis, the ship's cook on that crossing, but I have learned the basics of sailing well enough. I also discovered how treacherous the oceans can be, how storms can boil up from nowhere to kill crew and passenger alike.

My friend Francis was one of them, his life taken by a spar that fell on him during a wicked tempest. He wasn't the only one to die on the crossing that took me from Liverpool to Quebec, however. Migrants young and old perished in the hold of the ship from disease. Yes. I know my way around a ship and I have no desire to return to one — at least without my sister. "My sailing days are behind me," I tell him.

He doesn't give up. "We could always use a good hand on board the *Pelican*. Name's Robert, I'm her mate. We carry goods, bound for Valetta. Are you sure, lad? The Mediterranean is a good bit warmer than England this time of year. It's worth it, to feel the heat of the sun on your face, even with Napoleon's fleet out there!"

"Nae, but thank ye," I say, "though if I ever do want to sail again I know who ..."

"The press gang! Run for it!"

The sailor's words are cut off abruptly by the cry. Chaos

erupts in the pub. Men flee, upturning tables in their hurry to escape. The sailor I'd been talking to not five seconds ago is gone, vanished in the throng of seamen running for the exits.

I join them in the panic. I know what press gangs are. They work for the Royal Navy, recruiting men by force to serve on the warships of the fleet. We are at war with France after all; the Royal Navy is in desperate need of sailors and will find them anyway they can.

The Royal Navy patrols all the oceans of the world, with ships and bases as far as Africa, South America and New Zealand. If I'm captured by the group of large men who've barged into the pub, swinging large clubs, knocking men out then slapping them in manacles, it could be years before I get to search for my sister.

If I ever do.

I'm a fast runner, surely able to outrun any of the press gang, but in the tight space of the pub, with tables, chairs and frightened sailors blocking my way, my speed serves me no good at all as I slowly fight my way towards the door. Soon I'm twenty feet from freedom, then ten as the entry-way looms into view.

The door is five feet away, and wide open. In less than a second I'll be through it, out onto the open street where I'll be able to speed away. I cross through the threshold, about to stretch out my legs and sprint to safety, when I see a sudden flash of movement from the corner of my eye.

"I've got you now!" a man yells triumphantly. There are more of the pressers here, waiting in ambush as the rest of the gang herds us right towards them.

I try vainly to change direction. Perhaps if the cobbles were dry I would have made it, but a light spring rain is falling, making the road slippery. I stumble and slip on the wet stones, lose my balance and fall heavily to the street.

I struggle to get to my feet, to scrabble up off the cobbles but before I can stand up, the press gang is upon me. "Fair pay for your service," a man says, flipping what looks like a piece of silver onto my chest. Beside him another man raises a club.

"Welcome to the Royal Navy," he says and the last thing I see before my world goes black is his grinning face and the club that flies through the air towards me.

Chapter 7

"GOOD HEAVENS! Duncan Scott! I never thought I'd see you again, especially in these circumstances." My eyes reluctantly flutter open at the sound, head throbbing painfully from the blow. I know that voice, have heard it before, but in my fog I can't place it until the blurred face leaning over me slowly comes into focus.

"Tom?" I say, recognizing the man but not quite believing who I'm seeing. Tom Jenkins, a large bear of a man with thick curly black hair, was a sailor on the ship that carried me across the Atlantic to Canada.

At first Tom was not terribly impressed by my presence on the *Sylph*. "Stowaway" he called me with disdain, but that changed during the storm, a terrible gale on the Atlantic that nearly sank us, and claimed the life of Francis, the ship's cook. It would have killed Tom as well, had I not saved him from being swept off the deck of the ship.

"What am I doing back on the *Sylph*?" The last thing I remember is the press gang. Now I'm climbing slowly up from the rough wooden deck of a ship's hold, my head throbbing from a solid whack of a billy club.

"You ain't on the *Sylph*, I'm afraid to tell you."

"Och. So where am I? A dinnae ken what happened."

"You, my friend, are locked up on the gun deck of a fifth-rate Royal Navy frigate. His Majesty's Ship *Cerberus*, to be exact. We're currently tied up at the Deptford Dockyard, but we'll be makin' our way down the Thames at the turn of the tide, if the scuttlebutt is right."

"Nae! I cannae be! This is a mistake! There must be some way off!" I'm so close to finding Libby after all this time. I can't believe this has happened.

"Steady yourself, mate," Tom whispers. "You don't want to bring attention to yourself. You're a pressed man, a waister, as far as everyone else on board is concerned, the lowest of the low on a naval vessel. Your life will be miserable if you get on the bad side of the officers, and even worse if the men don't like you."

I take a breath to compose myself. No doubt Tom is right; to mark myself as a troublemaker will cause me no end of grief. "How did ye end up here, Tom?" I ask.

"I took the King's Shillin', much the same way you did."

"The King's what?" I'm not sure if I heard him correctly as I run my hand through my blood-crusted hair and feel an egg-sized lump on the back of my throbbing skull.

Fair pay for your service. I remember now what the presser said before clubbing me, the piece of silver I saw.

"The coin he gave me before knocking me out. That was the King's Shilling?"

"Aye," says Tom ruefully. "Some pressmen club sailors on the head and drag 'em aboard, like what happened to you. Not subtle but effective. Others slip the coin into a sailor's ale. When he drinks it? There's that damned piece of silver at the bottom of the mug. The King's Shillin', an acceptance of pay to serve in the Royal Navy, though no such trick was needed to get me.

"After you left us in Quebec, we picked up a load of sugar in Jamaica, just as Cap'n Smith said we would. We were on route back to Liverpool, but before we made port, *Cerberus* pulled up alongside.

"'King George needs sailors', they said, pointing their muskets at us. Before you know it, me and several of the other lads are in the Royal Navy, in exchange for a handful of pressed men from the *Cerberus* and a few coins. Cap'n Smith got the worse end of that trade, I can tell you. I've been here ever since."

"Why haven't ye left?" I ask. "Surely ye've had opportunity to do so?"

"For a while I thought about jumpin' ship," Tom admits. "But I have to say that I was getting a little tired of the Atlantic trade. Besides, we've had many grand adventures on *Cerberus*, my seamanship's improved beyond measure, and though the pay's not as good as it is in the merchant navy, we get a share in any French ship we take as a prize. In a year or two I'll leave and be more'n ready to master my own boat."

Then Tom says something unexpected. "Besides, I never much thought about it before, but there's somethin' to be said about doin' one's duty for King and Empire. If Boney has his way, he'll overrun England. I'm protectin' the country from him and glad to do it."

"Do ye ken where this ship is sailing to?" With my Scottish background, I don't share my friend's same patriotic stirrings and am praying we aren't about to embark to the Spanish Main or the South Pacific. If we do, it will be years until I return to England, if at all. After so long, to have come this close to finding my sister and have my hopes dashed like this? I want to scream.

"Not for sure," Tom says. "Officers don't tell us regular sailors much, but I was talkin' to the bosun before you and the others came on board last night, and he seems to think we're heading for the Baltic to fight the Russians. They've signed a peace treaty with Napoleon and have declared war on us."

"Where's the Baltic?" I've not heard of this sea, and am

struggling to keep my calm, to keep my wits about me until I can find a way to get off this ship.

"The Baltic's a sea by Sweden. A week or two sailin' north. From what I hear, there's been a rash of attacks against English shippin' by the Russians. It may not have been what you were expectin', Duncan, but you're off to do battle with the largest country on earth!"

Chapter 8

IT IS THEN I REALIZE I've lost some very important things. "Tom, I was wearing a black cloak when the pressers took me. Do ye ken were it is?" I'm not concerned about the cloak but rather with the money I've sewed within it.

"Sorry, Duncan. I was on watch when they brought you and the other unfortunate fellows below decks last night. All you had is what you're wearin' now."

"And my knife? The one ye gave me?" It's no longer on my waist.

"Knife? What knife are you on about?"

"Dinnae ye remember?" I say. "Back on the *Sylph*. Ye gave me some gear of an old shipmate of yers who died, including his knife."

"You still had *that* knife? After all this time?" Tom sounds very surprised to learn that.

"Aye," I say glumly, "until last night. I carried that blade across an entire continent. All the way to the Pacific. I killed a man with it as well," I say. "I had no choice. He was about to kill me and a companion."

"You have had some adventures, haven't you?" says Tom. He is sympathetic to my plight. "That old knife is gone as well, no doubt. The pressers get paid well for their work, but they always like to collect a little bonus. You'll never see it again, I'm afraid. Speaking of bonuses, check your pockets while you're at it. I'm curious to know if that shilling is still in your possession."

I stick my hands into my pockets, turning the lining inside out to reveal nothing. "They took that back as well. Does that mean I don't have to join the Navy?"

Tom laughs ruefully. "That's rubbing salt into a wound for certain. Sorry, Duncan, that ain't how it works. You're stuck on board for now." Tom reaches for his waist. "Take this instead," he says, passing me another knife, one with a hand-carved bone handle in a leather scabbard.

"Nae, 'tis yers. I had the last one ye gave me stolen."

"Don't worry," he says. "I've another. Remember what I told you last time? 'A sharp blade is good to have on board a ship. There are things out here other than waves that can kill you.'"

I take the knife, pull it out of the scabbard and check the

blade. The metal is dull grey but as sharp as a razor. "Thank ye, Tom. Again."

Then I run my hands along the waist of my trousers and feel the comforting shapes of the coins. Tom sees me do it. He is no fool and quickly realizes why I am so upset about losing my cloak.

"You had coins sewn in it as well as your trousers, didn't you?"

"My wages fer three years of work in the North West Company. Half was in my cloak." I'm angry beyond words. I've been kidnapped, turned over to the Royal Navy, been robbed, and worst of all, my chance of finding Libby has been taken from me as well.

"But you're still alive and half remains, so I'd be quiet about it or you'll lose that too," Tom advises. "You'll be gettin' your uniform soon enough. When you do, move your money to your new trousers."

"Uniform?"

"You're in the Royal Navy now. Look at me." Tom wears white canvas trousers held up with a braided rope belt, a grey-and-blue striped shirt and a blue jacket.

"It's quite the proper outfit, ain't it? Red vest, black kerchief, and tarred straw hat as well. Regular sailor's clothes ain't as fancy as an officer's, but Captain Whitby does like us looking smart."

* * *

"All hands!" yells someone as Tom and the other sailors snap smartly to attention.

"Stand straight, Duncan," Tom whispers. "Lieutenant Murray is comin' into the hold to inspect his new crew. He won't have much good to say about pressed men if experience means anythin', so mind yourself — and your tongue — or you'll likely to get the lash."

"Bloody landsmen," snorts First Lieutenant George Murray, second in command of HMS *Cerberus*, as he inspects the two dozen of us pressed into reluctant service.

The lieutenant wears a uniform much more impressive than the men's. His blue coat is longer, adorned with brass buttons and on his head is a black, three-pointed hat.

"What's your name, lubber?" Murray asks me, his face mere inches from my own.

"Stuart, Sir," I reply, keeping enough wits to remember the name I've been travelling under. "John Stuart, from Scotland."

"I can bloody well tell where you're from by the way you butcher the King's English, Stuart," Murray says sharply.

"Sir?" says Tom politely. He'd looked confused when I called myself John Stuart, but my friend knows why I left England in the first place and plays along.

"What is it, Jenkins?"

"If I may, Sir, John here's no lubber. We sailed together on the Atlantic crossing. He's not spent time in the riggin', but he's a good cook, and a half-decent deckhand as well."

The scowl leaves Murray's face, if only for a minute. "Well then," he says with some satisfaction, "the rest of this lot may be a waste of skin, but the pressers have done something right with him by the sounds of things. We've no use for another bloody cook, but an experienced deckhand always has a place on board."

"If it pleases you, Sir," Tom continues, "put Stuart on my watch. We've worked together before. I would be happy to show him the ropes, as it were."

Murray nods in agreement then moves on to the other pressed men, asking them each questions about their prior experience. Judging by the foul language that flies from his lips, none seem to meet his standard of seamanship. Inspection over, Murray turns on his heels and leaves the hold, back to whatever tasks he has above decks.

"Thank ye," I tell Tom, well aware of the huge service he's done me.

"Don't worry about it," he replies. "Just learn as much as you can, and do it quickly. You're a half-decent deckhand after all, no matter what name you're going by. You don't want anyone to think otherwise."

Chapter 9

"THIS CANNAE BE happening to me, Tom," I lament after changing into my ship's uniform. I am so close to finding my sister that to have been captured and handed over to the Royal Navy infuriates me nearly to tears.

Tom tries to console me. "It ain't that bad, Duncan. Most likely we'll be in the Baltic for only a month or two. The real danger to the Empire is what's left of Napoleon's fleet, and they sail in the Mediterranean and the North Sea. You'll have plenty of opportunities to slip off the ship and find your sister later."

"And be declared a traitor, then be hanged fer my troubles if caught? Nae, thank ye very much. I'm already a fugitive, if ye recall."

To my surprise Tom laughs. "Have no fear of that. The Army was looking for Duncan Scott, not John Stuart, and Duncan Scott is dead and long forgotten. As for the Royal Navy? We're conscripts, you and I. If a regular sailor deserts, they'll swing from the yardarm for sure, if caught. Pressed men? We may get a floggin' from the cap'n for good measure, but then we'll get thrown back into service until the ship sails back to London and we get paid off."

Suddenly the loud shrill of a pipe echoes through the hold. "Ahoy! All hands!" a voice cries.

"The tide's turned," says Tom. "Time to head to sea. We've been refittin' and victuallin' the ship for the last several months. All we needed was a sufficient crew. And thanks to the press gang," Tom says with some sympathy, "that need has been filled. Time to go above decks and say goodbye to England — at least for a little while."

The crew of *Cerberus* lines up along the rails as we slip from the pier and out into the river. The current is strong, and coupled with the ebbing tide, we have no difficulty travelling quickly downstream.

As we drift down the Thames I take stock of *Cerberus* for the first time. She is the largest ship I've ever seen, let alone sailed on.

She is a three-masted frigate, with a black hull and a tan keel, a strong ship, made from British oak and elm. Her sails are furled tightly to the spars. With the current and tide taking us downstream, the quartermaster needs no wind. He stands the helm, steering the ship, keeping it expertly in the middle of the river. Standing next to the quartermaster is Lieutenant Murray, and another officer who Tom says is Captain Whitby, the undisputed commander of *Cerberus*.

I stand beside Tom, on the deck between the mainmast and the foremast. I look down to the water. The river doesn't seem too far below me, certainly close enough for me to jump.

The bank is only thirty yards or so away, full of busy streets and buildings. There are a score of places to hide onshore. If I can make it. My mind races. I'm a good swimmer, perhaps I won't have to wait several months to continue my search for Libby after all.

"Don't even think about it, mate," whispers Tom, as if he can read my mind. "You wouldn't reach the bank. She don't look it but the Thames is a treacherous river when the tide runs. Between the currents and the cold you wouldn't stand a chance."

Another pressed sailor who came on board with me last night, George something or other, doesn't heed Tom's warning. "To blazes with the Royal Navy!" he suddenly shouts, climbing up and over the bulwark. Before anyone can stop him, he launches himself over the side of the ship, hitting the brown water below with a splash.

"Man overboard!" cries a sailor. On the quarterdeck Lieutenant Murray looks over to Captain Whitby. The captain shakes his head slightly, the motion barely visible.

"Hold your course," says Murray. "We couldn't reach him

in time, even if we wanted to. This man has chosen his fate, let him live or die with the consequences."

George bobs helplessly on the river for a while then he slips underneath the surface, reappearing long enough to scream for assistance. "Help!" he begs, but as the *Cerberus* passes on, and he disappears under the water again, his cries are cut off. This time George doesn't reappear.

"I told you the current's too strong," Tom says. "You'll make it off this ship sure enough one day, but hopefully not like him."

Chapter 10

THE LAST RIVER I SAILED was the St. Lawrence, a very different waterway than the Thames. The Thames is a smaller, tamer river, a river of cities and commerce and, as it broadens into its own estuary, a river of small, tidy English farms and villages.

Vessels are everywhere. Barges carry their cargoes, small fishing smacks make their way to the English Channel and merchant ships are pulled up the river by rowboats. No matter who they are, all boats give wide berth to *Cerberus*.

The row of cannon that bristle from our sides, as well as the St. George's Ensign, a red cross on a white background with the Union Jack in the top left corner that flies proudly from the stern, clearly mark us as a warship of the Royal Navy, and a source of national pride.

The most powerful force on earth, the Royal Navy is the only thing that stands between England and the conquering armies of Napoleon. No matter what the people of England think of their kings, queens and prime ministers, the Royal Navy is the force that keeps them safe, and its ships and sailors hold a special place in the hearts of every English man, woman and child. As a Scot, however? I hate the very sight of that flag.

On the riverbank, just past the town of Gravesend, a number of boys stop their playing and salute us as we pass. Captain Whitby, still standing beside the helmsman, smartly salutes back, much to the pleasure of both the boys and men on board. "God bless England!" a boy cries.

"Huzzah! Give Boney what-for!" shouts another as the crew on deck roars their approval.

A mile past Gravesend, and with the river widening rapidly, Lieutenant Murray gives the order the crew has been waiting for. "All hands! Make sail!"

"You watch the topmen climb," says Tom. "I used to think I knew how to sail until I ended up in the Royal Navy. It's nearly 200 feet from the waterline to the top of the main-mast, twice the height of the *Sylph's* mast. The lads that go aloft are either the bravest or craziest men in the fleet."

Within seconds, the spars and rigging high above the deck swarm with sailors. Massive canvas sails are quickly unfurled as the deck crew hauls on lines and lanyards, and in less time than I think possible, sails blossom like white clouds from the masts, and the *Cerberus* surges forward, east into the English Channel and the open sea.

"Welcome to the Royal Navy," Tom says. "Wanted or not, you're in for the adventure of a lifetime."

Chapter 11

"AHOY! STARBOARD WATCH! Rouse out there, you sleepers! Lash and carry!" At the barked command and the sharp whistle that precedes it, I tumble out of my hammock. Along with the other men stirred from sleep, I hurriedly stash my hammock into the storage netting, then scramble up the hatchway to the deck to begin my watch.

At four in the morning, sunrise is still an hour away, but that doesn't prevent us from getting on with the day's work. The pressed men are given the most menial of chores, jobs that require no skill whatsoever. They man the pumps to empty out the bilge, tend to the pigs that are kept in a small sty below decks and help the cooks.

Thanks to Tom I work on the deck instead of below in the hold. I get to breathe in the fresh air and watch the ship rise and fall on the waves. But even then I have no time to enjoy the sights. "Get scrubbing!" orders a boatswain's mate as we fill the buckets and wash down the decking.

"I thought ye said I was about to embark on the adventure of a lifetime." The two of us are on our knees, large scrub brushes in our hands. "I'm naught but a scullery maid right now."

"It's hardly the most glamorous of duties, I give you that. At least we're at four bells. Only another two hours until we rest and the other watch takes over."

The crew is divided into two watches, named after the ship's sides. Ours is the starboard watch. We're on duty for four hours at a time. The ship's bell rings every half an hour, marking time, gaining a ring each time until we reach eight bells — the welcome sound of the end of watch.

"Wash the deck, swab it dry, polish the brightwork," I complain a week later. "Fer this Libby has to wait?"

"Gunnery practice tomorrow, though," Tom says, trying to cheer me up. "That's excitin', ain't it? Maybe even a chance to work in the rigging if you prove yourself."

I scoff at the suggestion. "Prove myself to the English? They're the reason my family died in the first place. I went halfway around the world to get away from the redcoats and now I've joined them."

"You're not a soldier; you're a sailor, Duncan," Tom corrects me, but the look on my face tells him I see little difference between the two.

"Three years ago the British Army tried to kill me, chased me out of England, took me from the only family I had left. The Royal Navy has done the same as well. Soldiers, sailors, marines: it makes little difference to me the colour of the uniform."

On board *Cerberus*, the sailors, both common man and officer, wear blue, but twenty others dress in the red coats I've come to despise, though I learn that they are not soldiers but instead members of the Royal Marines.

"You're not the only one who don't care for the Marines," admits Tom. "Many of the lads think 'em a lazy lot, not helpin' with the sailin', just loungin' about, waitin' for action."

"That's because they *are* lounging about the ship, admiring themselves in their uniforms when we work like slaves," I grouse. "And how many times does this damned deck need swabbing?"

"Maybe you're right," says Tom, "but when it comes to a battle we'll be glad to have 'em in the fighting tops. Armed to the teeth they are, with their swords, flintlocks, pistols and grenades. One Marine is worth twenty regular sailors in a fight."

"Grenade? A dinnae ken that word."

"Grenades are a nasty bit of business," Tom explains. "See that Marine there, with the bandolier across his chest? Those are grenades."

The Marine Tom refers to is a tough-looking fellow standing watch on the deck. What Tom calls a bandolier is a belt he wears over his shoulder with several round metal objects, each about the size of a large apple attached to it. "What do they do?" I ask Tom.

"They're bombs. Metal containers filled with gunpowder with fuses stickin' out of the ends. Light the fuse, throw it at whatever or whoever you want to blow up then duck and cover."

"They sound very dangerous for such small-looking things."

"You don't know the half of it," he says. "I've seen 'em in action. When the bullets and cannonballs start firin', ain't nobody I'd rather have at my back than a Royal Marine loaded up with grenades. When we find the Russians you'll see what I mean soon enough."

Chapter 12

EIGHT BELLS SOUND across the *Cerberus* as the starboard watch stands down. "Not exactly steak and egg is it?" says Dutch, as we sit down to eat on the gun deck. Our meal is a mush made of oatmeal and raisins, called burgoo.

We wash it down with Scotch coffee, which despite its name is not coffee at all, but a mixture of hot water, burned bread and sugar. "At least it ain't mealy biscuits and salt pork yet," says Little Fred. "They save that for the back half of the trip."

Each watch is broken down into groups of eight men or so, called messes. In the week since I've been on board, the men in our mess have become close friends and have chosen Tom as our unelected leader.

There are only seven of us, each with a nickname. Tom is called Bull because of his size and strength. Morris and Little from Norwich were fishermen, friends before joining the Royal Navy. We call them Big Fred and Little Fred respectively: Morris because of his size, Fred because of his last name.

Samuel Akker, a young man with thin blond hair, is a Londoner, though his family comes from Amsterdam originally. His nickname, of course, is Dutch. Robert Adams, a fellow Scot from Edinburgh, is called Haggis.

The last man in our watch, William MacDonald, is from Halifax, in Nova Scotia. He's a couple of years older than me but has been in the Royal Navy since he was fifteen. We call him Yankee Bill because even though he's never been to the United States, Bill's accent is flat, like Simon Fraser's, in fact.

Then there's me. I'm now called Trap. In the course of our conversations, I've told the men about my experiences in the wilds of North America with the North West Company. Yankee Bill in particular was most impressed. He knows all about Canada, the Nor'Westers and the fur trade, and has even been to Montreal.

"You think the topmen are crazy?" he says to the other lads. "The fur traders our new friend travelled with are absolutely mad. To go through those wild lands with little more than a flintlock for protection? Trap must have gone crazy himself out there!"

Our four hours of rest passes quickly, and our watch begins again. Reluctantly we climb up onto the deck, knowing full well what the next four hours will bring. There's always wood to scrub and brass to clean, and then there is our sailing duty as well.

* * *

Cerberus is travelling north by northeast, but the winds blow from the northwest. We can't sail in a straight line because of it and are required to tack, to sail in a zigzag manner against the wind. On this watch it is our turn to man the ship's lines.

"Ready ho!" cries Second Lieutenant Wilson from the quarterdeck. The topmen high in the rigging stand ready to pull in sails while we are in the bow, working the lines on the foresails, ready to heave them in on command.

"Put the helm down!" orders the helmsman as the ship swings across the wind.

"Helm's a'lee!" Wilson shouts.

"Mainsail haul!" cries the helmsman in response.

"Pull with all your might, lads," says Tom. We wrench hard on the lines, hoisting the sails until the wind catches them and they billow, filled with fresh North Sea wind.

"Quick lads, be sharp with the lines," Tom warns. "Puddin's coming this way."

Midshipman Benjamin Figg walks the forecastle imperiously, scowling down on us as if he was the Admiral of the Fleet. Figg is my age, perhaps a year younger. He's a midshipman, a "young gentleman" as they're called in the Royal

Navy, a boy from a prominent family seeking a commission.

Midshipman Figg is also an unfortunate-looking person. It isn't that he's fat; it's more that he has no shape, no firmness to his body at all. He's soft, like a jellyfish or a pudding poured into a uniform, with thin brown hair, a prominent nose and no chin.

Second Lieutenant Wilson is in charge of the starboard watch, but he leaves much of the day-to-day tasks to Pudding — much to our regret. We called him Figgy Pudding at first, which quickly shortened to Pudding. Not to Figg's face, of course. We'd have been tied to the mainmast and flogged in front of the entire crew for such an affront.

It was Dutch who'd come up with the name. "Pudding" fit perfectly, and soon the entire watch referred to Midshipman Figg as such. Even some of the junior officers call him that as well.

The benefit of their rank allows them to say it to his face, which absolutely infuriates Midshipman Figg, though there is nothing he could do about it. It has become his mission to discover the source, and somehow, quite correctly, Figg suspects us.

"Ahoy! You there, sailor!" Figg shouts. "Avast!"

"He's talking to you, Trap," says Yankee Bill apologetically. I have a line in my hand, and am pulling it tight, wrapping it around a cleat. I hold fast as Pudding approaches.

"What the blazes do you think you're doing, sailor?" Pudding demands.

"I just wrapped the line around the cleat," I say respectfully.

"You call these lines taut?" Pudding stares up the foremast. "Useless waisters, the lot of you."

"I'm sorry, Sir, but I don't see nothin' wrong with the lines," says Tom, coming to my defence. "We've left no slack, nor are any lines tangled."

Tom is right, of course, but it doesn't seem to satisfy Midshipman Figg. In fact, his face glows red at the nerve of Tom saying anything at all to him.

"You mind your cheek, sailor! Bosun Watson!" Figg commands.

The bosun is a warrant officer. He is not commissioned like the lieutenants or Captain Whitby but has earned his place through skill and merit. His job is to assign the deck crews our tasks and supervise us closely.

"Sir?" says Watson, saluting Figg crisply.

"These lubbers know nothing about seamanship, especially the large one with the big mouth. I want them both scrubbing the deck until the wood shines, their fingers bleed, and they learn to respect their betters. Do you hear me?"

"Aye, Sir. Very well, Sir!" Watson replies. "You heard the midshipman! Brushes, buckets and swabs!"

With a smile on his face Figg takes his leave and returns to the quarterdeck. "The lines were fine," I say, getting down on my knees, brush in hand. The deck is hard, my knees are bruised and cut from the hours I've spent scrubbing, and the water stings my blistered fingers. The last thing the deck — or I — need is more scrubbing.

"It ain't about the lines," Tom says. "Puddin's just showing us he's in charge. There's a person like Figg on every ship in the Royal Navy. Stay out of his way and he won't bother you. Besides, how much harm can one man really do?"

I remember my journey with Simon Fraser and La Malice. The murderous voyageur nearly killed me twice, caused a mutiny and almost killed the leader of our expedition. "More than ye may think, Bull. Trust me," I say, "I ken first-hand how much harm one bad man can do."

Chapter 13

"RUN OUT THE GUNS, and fire on my command," says Warrant Officer Henry Rowe, chief gunner of the HMS *Cerberus*. Rowe is the senior warrant officer on board, a career sailor from Ipswich in charge of all of the ship's guns, ammunition and powder.

My heart pounds with anticipation. We've been in the belly of the ship, on the gun deck for several hours now, doing dry runs with the twenty-six cannons. Now we are about to fire them for real. My messmates and I are in charge of the stern-most gun on the starboard side of the ship. Tom is our gun captain, while the rest of us have other duties.

"Why is the gun deck painted red?" I ask, taking my position beside the cannon.

"That's to mask the sight of our blood," says Yankee Bill. "The captain wouldn't want us going all squeamish in the middle of the battle, would he?"

"Them buckets against the bulwarks, Trap. You see 'em?" adds Haggis.

"Aye, what of them?"

"Filled with sand, they are. When we go to war for real, we'll spread it around the guns so we don't slip in our own blood. We'll also light the lanterns that hang above the guns when it comes to the real thing. Without them, when the twenty-six guns start firing you won't see your hand in front of your face for all the smoke."

Rowe takes out his pocket watch as silence settles on the gun deck. All we can hear is the gentle tick of his watch, our own breath and the sea bubbling below the open gun ports.

"Level your gun!" Rowe orders. Haggis and Yankee Bill lift up the breech of the gun with large wooden handspikes. Their job is to raise and lower the cannon until it is in its proper position. When the breech, the rear of the cannon, is level with the deck, Tom sticks a wooden brace under the breech to hold it in place.

"Load with cartridge!" At Rowe's order, Little Fred stuffs a canvas bag full of gunpowder into the barrel of the gun, followed by a wad of cloth. This is where I go to work. I am the sponger. My first duty is to take a ramrod and tamp the bag of gunpowder and the wad right into the barrel of the cannon.

"Is it in?" I nervously ask, knowing the gun won't fire if I haven't done my job correctly. Tom takes a thin copper wire and sticks it through the vent hole in the breech.

He nods. "Wire's pierced the bag proper. It's right where it needs to be."

Almost despite himself, Pudding grunts in approval. He is behind us, watching carefully. There are twenty-six gun crews training today, a full complement, but to nobody's surprise Figg has decided to stand near us, watching everything we do with his watery eyes.

"Shot and wad your gun!" cries Rowe, the second-to-last order before we fire. On command, Big Fred picks up one of the large iron balls and rolls it down the barrel. Little Fred inserts a cloth wad, then I tamp the ball and wad tightly against the bag of shot.

"Right, lads," whispers Tom. "Let's show 'em how we shoot." Rowe runs his eye up and down the side of the ship. When he is confident all are ready, he gives his next command. "Roll out your gun!"

"Heave!" cries Tom. The cannon on the gun deck are 18-pounders, named after the weight of the cannonballs. With their long brass barrels and the wheels and tackle they are built on, each gun weighs more than two thousand pounds.

The entire gun crew puts our shoulders to the cannon. We push as hard as we can, the heavy weapon slowly moving forward until the tackle is flush against the bulwark, the barrel poking through the open gun port.

"You there!" Rowe says to the crew next to us. "Your gun's

too far back. Shove it forward another foot. Good," he says when they make the adjustment. "Prepare to fire, but stand to the side unless you want to lose your feet, your hands and whatever other appendages you've grown accustomed to!"

We wait to shoot though we have nothing to aim at but the gently rolling sea. "Wait for the down roll," Rowe says. The seas are light but the swells are still large enough for the ship to rise and fall, and when we roll down with the wave, Master Rowe gives the final order.

"Fire!" he cries.

Tom and the other gun captains pull sharply back on lanyards connected to the flintlock hammers, and the gun deck erupts in smoke and noise. The cannons roll back on their iron trucks with terrific force, stopping only when the thick ropes that attach them to the sides of the ship stretch tight against their weight, stopping their momentum.

Ears ringing from the massive din, I take another ramrod from Dutch, this one with a damp sponge attached to its end, then run it down the barrel, extinguishing any hot sparks, cleaning out unburned pieces of wadding.

If this had been a real battle, the ship's powder monkeys, lads as young as ten, would be running between the gun deck and orlop deck, two decks below us, to the shot lockers where the gunpowder is secured.

"Not bad," says Rowe, looking at his watch. Not bad is a tremendous compliment from the gunner. Tom knows it and he flushes with pride. Figg on the other hand looks like he is sucking on a lemon.

"Three minutes that took, but when I'm done with you lot, you'll be firing three shots in five minutes, and the Russian Navy will tremble when they see our sails!"

When our cheers subside, Rowe makes a surprising announcement. "We're not done yet. Captain Whitby wants his gun crews to be the best in the fleet. As we speak, a ship's boat is towing a target off the starboard bow. They'll let it loose and as it floats past, each gun crew will have a chance to blow it to blazes. The crew that hits the target will receive an extra ration of grog at supper! Now get to your guns and make ready!"

"Three cheers for Cap'n Whitby!" someone cries.

"Huzzah! Huzzah! Huzzah!" we reply in unison, before turning our attention back to our 18-pounder.

"Right lads," whispers Tom. "I can taste that grog already. Let's show Rowe and Puddin' how real sailors can shoot."

Chapter 14

ONE HUNDRED YARDS from *Cerberus,* the ship's longboat tows the target, a collection of a dozen empty water barrels, tied together with netting. We watch through the gun port as one of the sailors in the boat cuts the tow rope and sets the makeshift target loose.

The barrels approach and the gun in the bow fires. When the smoke clears, we see the target completely unharmed, the ball splashing into the sea two hundred yards off target. "Useless!" says Rowe in derision. "Far too high!"

The next gun crew makes adjustments and fires as the barrels come into view. They are closer, but still miss by fifty yards, their shot going high and to the right.

The next three guns all miss, though they each come closer in turn. The misses are met with good-natured jeers and catcalls.

The crew two guns from us strike first. They hit a barrel on the edge of the target, blowing it to smithereens, but the netting holds and, bobbing roughly from the glancing blow, the target approaches. "Not bad," says Rowe approvingly. "Let's see if you remaining lot can finish the job."

The gun to our immediate right fires. It is a close miss, the ball hitting the water just a few feet in front of the barrels. The ball kicks up a wave and the barrels bob violently on the water but remain untouched.

"Steady lads, steady," says Tom, staring keenly down the cannon. "A littler higher," he orders, and Yankee Bill and Haggis raise the gun slightly with their handspikes.

"On the down roll," he says, more to himself than anyone else. Tom waits patiently until the ship rolls gently downward.

"Now!" cries Tom, and the cannon fills the gun port as he deftly pulls the lanyard. Our gun erupts in flame. Smoke billows around us, but through it I see that our target has been smashed into a million splinters.

"Well done!" says Rowe as we congratulate Tom, slapping him smartly on the back.

"'Tis much like shooting a very large pistol," I tell Tom.

"What's that you said, waister?" Pudding suddenly interrupts our celebrations, and pushes his way towards me.

"What the devil do you know about shooting pistols? More than you know about how to haul lines and sheets, I hope!"

The gun deck falls silent as the men wait my response. "Sir, when I was in Canada I was taught to shoot by the voyageurs. I crossed North America and back with a pistol at my side."

Pudding laughs, a high-pitched nasally giggle. "So the Highlander learned how to shoot in a land of savages, did he? This I must see! Master Rowe, set up a target. Let us all find out how well our little Scottish friend knows his pistols."

"Sir," says Rowe deferentially to Second Lieutenant Wilson who has been watching us train from a corner of the gun deck, "I don't think it's wise to fire live pistols below decks, not with the powder kegs and such. Perhaps this little competition should occur on the main deck above."

"Nonsense, gunner," says Wilson. "Our hull is built of solid English oak, made to stop a cannonball. I hardly think a pistol shot will sink us. Besides," he adds with a grin, "I believe I'd like to see this myself."

"Yes," Pudding sneers. "Let us see how the whelp shoots." With a nod from Wilson, Rowe sets a pewter drinking mug on a table. "We'll shoot from twenty paces," says Figg, taking his pistol out of his belt.

"I dinnae have a pistol, Sir," I say, my ears stinging from the rebuke.

Whelp.

That was what La Malice called me on the first day I arrived in Fort St. James, the day I splashed him with my paddle. I've not heard that word for a long time. To be called that name by a boy younger than I am makes my blood boil.

"Not to worry, waister," Figg says. "I'll shoot first then lend you mine. I wouldn't want you to weasel your way out of this."

Figg and I stand in the middle of the deck, the men cramming excitedly behind us. Figg steps up, pistol in hand and aims at the mug. "Watch and learn how an English gentleman does it."

He pulls the trigger. The pistol cracks loudly and the ball whizzes past the mug, so close it wobbles as the small lead shot flies past, burying itself into the side of the ship with a thud.

Judging by the sour look on Pudding's face, he'd not expected to miss. "Your turn, landsman," he spits, handing me his pistol and bag of shot and powder. "Let's see if you can do any better."

I reload, tamping down the powder and ball. It's been an age since I've fired a pistol, not since I was on the lower reaches of Fraser's River, with the Musqueam chasing after me with their arrows and spears.

"A wise man would miss this shot," whispers Tom. "Puddin' won't forgive a comeuppance."

"Aye," I reply, "mayhaps a wise man would."

I used to be rash, prone to making hot-headed decisions, choices that cost me dearly when I was younger. I know exactly what I should do, but Pudding has called me out, insulted me in front of my friends. That will not stand.

I take careful aim and squeeze the trigger gently. *Bang.* The mug bounces sharply off the table, holed clear through by the ball. The crew erupts in applause, with even Rowe and Second Lieutenant Wilson cheering.

"Yer pistol, my laird," I say deferentially, handing Figg back his gun. The midshipman scowls, his cheeks glowing red as he snatches the pistol, tucks it back into his belt and storms off.

"You've made an enemy of Puddin' and you'll come to rue that, I reckon," Tom says, shaking his head. "I thought I said a wise man would miss?"

"Aye, ye did," I say, "but I've not often been accused o' being one o' them before."

Chapter 15

"THAT'S JUTLAND," says Tom as a faint headland appears to the east, a low, long peninsula projecting into the grey sea. "The cap'n will be having us on a war footin' soon as we enter the Skagerrak, the strait that leads us into the Baltic. The Baltic's a Russian lake; we'll be surrounded by enemies and we'd best be on our toes."

We've been at sea for two weeks. Sailing directly to the Baltic would have taken *Cerberus* less than a week, but Captain Whitby has taken his time, allowing us to practise on the guns and the sails in anticipation of the coming fight.

"When was yer first fight?" I ask Tom. As we near enemy territory, my excitement is rising.

"Last year in the West Indies, just after I left the *Sylph*. We had a different cap'n then, Cap'n Selby," says Tom. "He commanded *Cerberus* for five years before he was given a newer ship. Cap'n Whitby was commissioned during our refit. Good men both. I've not seen Whitby under fire yet, but he has a heart of oak, I think. He'll stand firm."

"What's it like? Battle, I mean?" I've been in a few skirmishes, have shot my gun in anger, even killed a man, but my experiences pale in comparison to engaging in warfare with the firepower we have on board.

"Oh, Trap! I've never been so terrified, so frightened, yet so exhilarated and alive in all my days! We were blockadin' off Guadeloupe, in the Caribbean. Cap'n Selby learned that some blasted French privateers were in port so he decided to do somethin' about it."

Tom's eyes gleam as he talks. "We took the island of Marie-Galante first. Cap'n landed a force of sailors and Royal Marines and they shot the French out of their batteries. You've seen how the Marines don't get much credit on board, but they're crack shots and hard men when there's a battle to be fought.

"After Marie-Galante we sailed north to this little flyspeck of an island, La Désirade. That was my first taste of real war. We traded shots with the French battery that guarded the harbour. Showed 'em what-for, too, blew the guns to pieces, captured the island and a French garrison. Took a poundin' though, we did."

"Did ye get hurt?" I ask Tom, and for just a second Tom's eyes darken.

"Me? No, but good men died that day. A few were mates of mine. Fine lads all, God rest their souls. You see things in battle that you can't unsee, if you know what I mean, Trap. Cannon fire can do terrible things to flesh. There's excitement to be sure, but war can be a horrible thing."

Tom falls silent for a moment or so, and when he speaks again I can tell he's choosing his words carefully. "I've been meanin' to ask you something since you came aboard, Trap, but haven't found the way to say it."

"Aye?" Tom has a serious tone I've not heard before.

"Your sister. It's been three years since you last saw her, right?"

"Almost to the day." An image of Libby's face pops into my head. At least the Libby I used to know. She would have grown into a fine young woman by now.

"Have you ever thought that maybe your fate and hers are meant to go different paths?"

"A dinnae ken yer meaning, Tom." Since that fateful day in Liverpool with the British Army breathing down my neck I've thought of precious little else but finding Libby. To suggest otherwise is something I've never once considered.

"I mean no disrespect, my friend. How old would your sister be now?"

"Almost twenty," I say. "Why?"

"Maybe it's because I'm a sailor. We're a superstitious lot,

I grant you, but it seems to me that life has other plans for you. Probably there'll be suitors for her soon, with a husband and children to follow. She will be fine, I know. Perhaps you should accept that you are both following different stars."

Maybe life has other plans for you.

My friend and travelling companion, Luc Lapointe, said the very same thing when we left Red River for Fort St. James. I fall silent as memories wash over me. Fate has certainly conspired to keep me from my sister. Maybe Tom is right. Perhaps I'm not meant to see her again after all.

A sudden hissed warning from Tom brings me back. "Trap! Look smart! Pudding's coming towards us."

"What the blazes does he want? We're not on watch." Tom and I were lazing in the waist as we talked, resting against one of the ship's boats, enjoying the late spring sun and warm westerly breeze. That we are not on duty doesn't seem to bother Pudding, however.

"Attention!" barks Pudding as he waddles quickly towards us. Tom and I quickly stand up to salute him. Since I bested him with his own pistol last week, Figg's not said two words to me, though I've felt his gaze burning into the back of my neck every time I see him.

"Lounging about are you, waisters?"

"Aye, Sir," Tom says, "just resting a bit before the dog watch." Figg ignores the response, staring up the mainmast as if he were looking for something.

"Tell me, my sharpshooting friend," he says to me. "Can you see that rip in the moonsail?"

The moonsail is the topmost sail in the rigging, nearly two hundred feet above the deck. "Nae, Sir," I say, squinting into the sky. "I cannae say I do."

"It looks fine to me too, Sir," adds Tom.

"Well I see a tear, Stuart," smirks Figg. "I order you to climb up the rigging and confirm the damage."

"But we're not on watch right now," Tom says. "Surely the lads on duty should do that."

"Are you questioning an order, sailor?" Figg's voice takes on a dangerous tone.

Tom does his best to be respectful. "No, Sir, it's just that we ain't on watch is all. Besides, the sails and rigging are topmen duties, not deckhands."

"I've given our fur-trader friend here an order," Figg says with a smirk. "Surely someone brave enough to traverse the wild with fur traders and savages can do something as simple as checking the rigging. Up you go, boy, and don't stop till you clear the topgallant."

"Sir." Tom's protests are more forceful this time. "Please, Stuart here has no experience in the rigging. It would be murder to send him up. Let me go."

"I don't believe I asked your opinion on the subject, sailor. You will shut your mouth and the boy will climb."

"Trap, don't." Tom's face now flushes with anger. "The sail's fine. Pudding's just trying to get back at you for besting him. This is madness."

"You impudent rascal!" screams Figg at the use of his hated nickname. "How dare you!" The midshipman pulls his sword from its scabbard, and waves it at Tom. "Mr. Collins! Master at Arms! There's an insubordinate wretch of a sailor refusing to follow orders! Clap him in irons!"

Robert Collins, *Cerberus'* master at arms, hurries over to Figg, along with two of his assistants. Collins is a warrant officer, in charge of enforcing ship's discipline and meting out punishment as needed.

"To the brig with him!" orders Figg, but Collins pauses for just a second. By now there's a large crowd of sailors watching. They see what's going on, have heard the order for me to climb, and the dark looks on their faces show their displeasure at Figg's actions. If a man could be killed by a look, Pudding would be dead multiple times.

"Stand down, the lot of you," says Tom, as Collins places his hands in irons. "I'll not have any man punished for my actions."

Our messmates and the other sailors reluctantly clear a path for Collins, who marches Tom off the deck. Tom is a well-liked member of the crew, hardworking, loyal to a fault. His treatment will not go down well with the men.

"Be careful, Trap," says Tom as he's bundled off the deck. "You're far too good a man to suffer at the hands of an incompetent, regardless of his rank."

"You'll be hanged for this, Jenkins," says Figg, a satisfied smile pasted on his jowly face. "And anyone who doesn't disperse will be whipped with the cat."

"You heard the midshipman," says Collins. "Clear off or

end up in the brig yourselves." At the command, the men slowly return to their stations, muttering to each other in quiet, unhappy tones.

"Now see to the moonsail," Figg says to me. "All the way to the top."

I don't like heights. Even before La Malice nearly tossed me to my death from the rope bridges high above Fraser's River, I'd not been fond of them. Now? I hate the notion of my feet leaving solid ground, but leave they will.

The moonsail is at the top of the mast, a very great distance from here. The mast is held in place with a series of vertical ropes called shrouds. The shrouds are connected by ratlines, ropes that act like the rungs of a ladder.

The topmen clamber up the ratlines and shrouds like squirrels, but I am no topman. In all the time I've spent aboard a ship, I've not climbed more than a few feet up a mast. Until now.

I take a deep breath, steady my nerves and begin to climb. At first, it is easier going than I'd thought, no harder than scaling a ladder. I make steady process, climbing slowly and surely towards the wooden platform about a third of the way up the mast.

"It's madness, you climbing up here," Jessop, one of the port watch topmen, says from above in the rigging. "That bloody sail is fine. I can see it from here. Everyone can."

"Bull said the same thing, but I dinnae ken if it made much difference with Midshipman Figg."

"I heard. Come on then, lad, let's get this over with. Go through the lubber's hole when you reach the top. I don't want you climbing the futtocks and falling. You're fifty feet up, more'n enough to kill you if you slip."

True topmen disdain the lubber's hole, the gap in the top used by the Royal Marines and other deck men when they come up to fire on enemy ships and sailors. Instead, topmen scramble up the futtocks, shrouds angled to get around the top to the point that sailors are nearly upside down for a few feet until they clear the top and reach the upper mast.

Gratefully, I squeeze through the lubber's hole and stand on the top, catching my breath. "Damn that Pudding," says Jessop, staring down at the midshipman. "He'll get someone killed before this trip is through. Take it slow and you'll be fine, lad," he says. "It's a straight shot up. Stay tight to the rigging. Don't look down. Take one foot at a time. Up and down in five minutes."

I thank Jessop for his help, collect my nerves and carry on. It may be a straight shot, but it's a straight shot of more than 150 feet into the sky, through a spider's web of lines, spars, sails and shrouds.

It doesn't help matters that the ship is moving. Not just side to side, but pitching gently, the bow rising and falling with the waves. What seems to be almost imperceptible motion on the deck is exaggerated a hundredfold as I climb. I heed Jessop's advice and keep my eyes focused on the moonsail, still thirty feet above me.

The wind whistles through the lines. The sails rustle as they fill with air, and the halyards and blocks smack against the mast, groaning and creaking as if it were alive.

Finally I clear the topgallant, the sail below the moonsail. To the east, the Jutland peninsula stretches out blue and brown as far as I can see. Seabirds wheel in the air. Birds are normal enough on the sea, although it's quite disconcerting to see a gull flying far below me.

There are no other sails, no sign of people for as far as I can see, and with the exception of the thin sliver of Danish coast miles to the east, the whole world is nothing but wind, sky and the slate-grey sea.

I reach my destination and inspect the moonsail. As Jessop said, and as Figg no doubt knew, it is in perfect shape, a square, billowing sheet of canvas, doing its job just as it should.

I start my way slowly back down to the deck when *Cerberus* pitches forward. I'm not expecting the sudden movement, and my foot slips on the ratline. My stomach flies up into my throat as my feet flail in the air for what seems like an eternity until they make contact with the ratlines.

I spend a moment or so trying to control my ragged breath, then, keeping my eyes fixed on the mast I continue down. Holding tight to the lines I make my way back to the top where I'm congratulated by Jessop who's been watching me anxiously.

"Not bad for a waister!" he says, slapping my back. "If you

want to join the real sailors up in the rigging, I'll take you under me wing anytime!"

"Thank ye, Mr. Jessop, but fer now I'm happy to keep my feet on the deck!" I climb through the lubber's hole, make my way quickly back to the deck and report to Figg. "The moonsail is fine, Sir," I say, my heart finally slowing.

"Silly me," says Figg. "I could have sworn I saw a tear. Carry on with your lounging then. You've got a few bells yet to lounge about before you start your watch and then bear witness to the punishment the captain will inflict upon your insubordinate friend. He'll be dangling from the yardarm for certain before this day is through. He won't live to see another sunset."

Chapter 16

"ALL HANDS WITNESS punishment!" shouts the bosun's mate as Collins brings Tom up to the deck. It is eleven o'clock in the morning, and I've spent the last few hours worrying about Tom and what will happen to him.

Pudding pledged that Tom would hang, but some of my messmates are not concerned about that near as much as I thought they would be.

"At worst he'll get three dozen lashes with the cat," says Haggis with authority. He would know. Haggis is the longest-serving sailor in our mess, and has seen more than a few men punished.

"Maybe, but it depends on what 'e's charged with," replies

Dutch. "As far as Puddin's concerned, Bull's guilty of muti-nous behaviour. That's an 'angin' for sure."

"True but the cap'n may 'ave other ideas, however," says Little Fred hopefully. "Insolence, disobedience, neglect of duty; who knows what 'e'll think up? Cap'n Whitby's proved 'imself a good man so far. I hope 'e shows mercy today."

The Royal Marine drummer beats us to quarters. Captain Whitby and the officers stand ready, in full uniform. Mid-shipman Figg stands next to them on the quarterdeck, a smug look on his face, clearly enjoying the misery he's caused. Captain Whitby gives Collins a subtle nod and the punishment begins.

"Rig the gratings!" orders Master Collins.

"He won't be hanged at least," whispers Bill with relief. "It's the cat-o'-nine-tails for certain."

"Like I said," says Haggis quietly. "Mercy or not, it won't be pretty."

"Silence in the waist!" yells Master Collins. We aren't the only ones muttering. The entire crew has assembled to wit-ness Tom's punishment, and the men are most unhappy. Figg was unpopular before this incident. Now? The mid-shipman is the most hated man on board.

Captain Whitby stands on the bridge and addresses the ship. "Seaman Tom Jenkins. You have been found guilty of insolence to an officer. Twelve lashes! Bosun's mate, lay on the flogging."

I'm confused to see that instead of being angered by the

punishment, the men seemed pleased, almost happy. Even the officers seem to be in agreement with the decision.

All that is, except for Midshipman Figg. His smug expression has disappeared, replaced by a sour look on his flabby face. "What's going on?" I ask Haggis. "Twelve lashes with the cat? 'Tis awful!"

"Nae, lad," says Haggis. "'Tis as much a punishment on Figg as it is Bull. Cap'n could have ordered six dozen lashes. Tom's a well-liked crewman; nobody wants to see him come to any unnecessary harm, including the officers."

"I told you Cap'n's a good man," adds Little Fred. "He's sending a message to the men to be respectful of their superiors as he must, but it's also a warning to the officers, especially that damned Pudding, to be mindful of how they treat us. Look at Figg. By the sour look on his face you'd think he was the one getting lashed."

The carpenter and his mates lift up one of the large wooden grates that cover the hatches and place it against the bulwarks.

"Strip to the waist, Jenkins," orders Collins, almost apologetically.

"Aye, master," replies Tom, taking off his jacket and shirt. Tom makes no effort to argue or fight. He leans up against the wood, raising his hands to make it easier for the bosun's mates to lash him to the grate with long leather straps.

"This ain't gonna be a picnic for Bull," says Dutch. "The cat can make an awful mess of a man's hide."

Tom is properly secured, and the flogging begins when the bosun's mate, a large, muscular man named Aldridge, removes the cat-o'-nine-tails from a red cotton bag. I feel sick when I see it. The cat is a rope-handled whip, some three feet long with nine tails made of knotted thin cord.

"Show us what yer made o', Bull," whispers Haggis as Aldridge gives the whip to Collins. The master at arms quickly drives the whip down on Tom's back. Tom grunts, but does not cry out, not about to give Pudding any satisfaction.

Nine cruel-looking welts immediately rise up on his back, and Tom doesn't have more than a few seconds to draw a breath when Collins strikes again.

By the third strike, blood is running freely down Tom's back, staining his trousers and the wooden decking. Collins, breathing heavily himself, runs the cat's tails through his fingers, removing small chunks of flesh from the knots.

Stroke after stroke rains down on Tom's back, and though he gasps with each lash he doesn't cry out, nor beg for mercy, though bits of his blood-flecked skin cover Collins and the men closest to him.

"Cut him down," orders Whitby after the twelfth lash. Tom's back is a mess of blood and gore, and I expect him to fall unconscious when the leather straps are sliced. Instead, Tom stays on his feet, wobbling slightly but upright nevertheless as he turns to the captain and salutes. It is only then that Tom falls to his knees.

Bill leads us towards Tom. "Let's go tend to our mate, lads."

We are Tom's messmates. It's our job to get him back to the gun deck, to tend his wounds. Before I disappear below, helping to carry what is now an unconscious Tom, I watch Captain Whitby take his leave of the quarterdeck, followed by an unhappy Figg.

The midshipman looks like a dog with its tail between his legs. While Tom was the one flogged, there's no doubt at all that it's Midshipman Figg who has been given the greater punishment.

Chapter 17

FOR A WEEK TOM lies on a makeshift canvas bed on the floor of the deck. When we are not on watch we take care of his wounds, washing the cruel stripes on his back with clean sea water. For the first two days after the whipping, Tom can't eat or drink, barely able to sip from the water-soaked sponge we place to his lips.

Once a day, just after we eat breakfast, Doctor Torrance, the ship's surgeon, a short round man with bushy sideburns and spectacles, attends to Tom as well. At any given time, more than a dozen men report to Torrance for sick call, but the doctor makes them wait until he has tended our friend.

Most have little more than seasickness or a fever, and

most are suspected of shirking their duty. Torrance dismisses most of their complaints, but he has sympathy for our mate. Tom's a good sailor, no shirker, and though no one argues with the decision to flog him, we know that Doctor Torrance, like everyone else on board, holds Pudding responsible.

"You'll be right as rain in a few weeks, Jenkins," says Torrance, as relieved as I am that Tom will recover. "Your mates have done a good job looking after you. There's not much I can do about the scars, unfortunately. You'll bear them for life like a lot of men in the fleet, but you've avoided infection and gangrene."

"I'm so sorry," I tell my friend when he is well enough to sit. Tom's back is horribly marked: long, red-crusted welts from his waist to his neck, dozens of them, all because he defended me. "'Tis my fault ye were flogged. I feel absolutely terrible."

Tom manages a smile for the first time in many days. "No, Trap, I owe these stripes to Pudding alone. Someday I will have the chance to pay him back for them."

We have more pressing concerns than revenge on Midshipman Figg, however. While Tom recovers, *Cerberus* passes stealthily through the Skagerrak Strait into Kattegat Bay. To our west lies the coast of Denmark. To the east, the low mountains of Sweden, both visible to the lookouts perched high up the masts, scanning the horizon anxiously for sails. While not in the Baltic proper, we are rapidly approaching its western reaches, and Russian ships could be anywhere.

"That's Amager Island ahead," says Yankee Bill. "I've seen it before. A few years ago I served on the *Ruby* under Cap'n Draper. We were part of the fleet that laid siege to Copenhagen. The Danes were all set to join the Russians and French, so we laid siege to the city to show them the error of their ways. Took dozens of ships from the Danes. Better off in our hands than used by Napoleon against us, don't you think?"

A few miles off Amager, *Cerberus* bears west, to Bill's approval. "Good thinking on the Cap'n's part. We're going the long way around, through the Great Belt instead of the Sound. The Sound's shorter, but we're much more likely to encounter Russians that way. We'll engage them soon enough, but it will be on our terms not theirs."

Mist and late spring rain envelop us as we enter the Great Belt, a narrow strait on the less-populated eastern side of Amager Island. The strait is a thin, treacherous passageway of water full of rocks and small islands, and we sail slowly for fear of running aground.

"Ten fathoms," cries a man on the port bow. The water around Amager is well-travelled by Royal Navy warships, but Captain Whitby takes no chances, ordering us to take soundings of the depth of the water. At best, to hit a reef or end up on a sandbar would be the end of Whitby's career. At worst? We'd be a helpless target for any prowling Russian ship.

"Masthead there!" comes the sudden cry from the lookout at the top of the foremast. The Marine drummer plays a quick, smart drum roll that echoes across the ship as all men, on watch or not, fly to their battle stations.

"Empty that bucket of sand around the gun and light the lantern, lads," says Tom when we get to our gun. He's moving slowly, and cannot bear the feeling of a shirt on his back, but Tom is at his station, nevertheless, much to the admiration of the crew. Lesser men would still be lying on their stomachs.

I struggle to control my shaking hands as we go about our tasks, loosing the gun, sanding the deck, and removing the wooden stopper that keeps sea water from entering the barrel. Down below in the magazine, the powder monkeys are standing by with shot, ready to keep us gunners well-supplied.

All across *Cerberus*, men are readying for war. Topside the Royal Marines are climbing into the fighting tops, tubs of water are being poured, and anything that can fly about the boat in a battle is stowed away.

On the mess deck directly below us, Doctor Torrance is readying his table in the midshipman's quarters, preparing his bone saws and knives. His job will be to cut off the remnants of the shattered limbs of any poor soul unlucky enough to be hit with cannon fire.

Gunner Rowe stands behind us, ready to give the order to fire. He will make the command once, then we are on our own, firing at whatever ship appears until the battle is over or we are dead.

Rowe has a determined, confident look, but Pudding, who stands beside him, shakes. I swear I can hear his knees knock as we wait expectantly.

Every sound seems exaggerated: the bubbling and gurgling

of the sea against the sides and keel of the ship, the murmured conversation of gun crews, the muted cough of a sailor, the creaking of the ship as we rise gently on the swells.

"Stand down!" comes the cry from above decks.

"Stand down!" commands Rowe.

"Why ain't we firing?" Big Fred asks.

"More'n likely the lookouts at the mastheads saw a whale and got spooked," says Dutch. "We'll find out when we go topsides."

When I am back on the main deck I see that our lookouts did indeed see another sail. Off the port bow a fishing smack sails towards us. Its crew no doubt as relieved as I that we didn't open fire, but as they pass by not ten yards away, I see their scowls and hard looks, and I am left with no doubt of their feelings towards the Royal Navy of Great Britain.

The sailors have been drinking as well as fishing by the looks of things. One lifts a brown bottle to his lips, drains whatever is left in it down his throat then throws the empty bottle overboard.

"Damn you English!" he yells at us. He moves unsteadily in his boat, his words slurred as he continues to throw insults our way, in both English and another language I don't understand.

Tom chuckles. "Not Russians. They're Danes by the sounds of things and well into their cups. Sticks and stones. Let the drunkard rail, the cap'n will ignore that just fine if that's all the lout does."

"They don't seem to like us very much," I say.

"I would think not, Trap. We were at war with them a few years back. The Royal Navy blew the tar out of Copenhagen, made the Danes sign a peace treaty, then took half the Danish Navy for our troubles. They weren't much happy about it, but they put quill to parchment and signed anyway. Peace treaty or not though, these particular Danes ain't shy about showing their true feelings."

The other Dane shouts at us as well as he climbs unsteadily to his feet, but not before he picks up a long object that at first I mistake for a stick of some sort.

Tom recognizes the thing for what it is before me. "No, mate!" he shouts to the Dane. "Put that musket down. No good will come of you waving that thing at us."

Goodness knows why they have a gun on their boat. Maybe they use it to shoot large fish before they land them. Perhaps there are pirates in the Baltic they fear.

Regardless of the reason, the Danish sailor doesn't heed Tom's warning. Their small vessel is only twenty yards away from our port midships when the Dane clumsily swings the rifle towards us, cocks the hammer and shoots.

The shot echoes over the water, smoke rising in a cloud about the man who pulled the trigger. Above me and to my right I hear the musket ball, an angry bee flying through the air before it thuds into the mainmast.

Captain Whitby's response comes instantly, in the shape of a sharp nod of his head to Lieutenant Gladding, the commanding officer of *Cerberus'* Royal Marine detachment.

Gladding is a tall man with short black hair and sharp features. He looks every inch a warrior, born to wear his red uniform. "Marines! Fire!" he commands.

"God save those fools below," says Tom sadly. "I told 'em not to shoot at us. Cap'n Whitby is a good man. He can laugh off an insult or two, but no cap'n of a ship of the line will abide coming under fire and not respond in kind."

In the tops, five Marines aim their own flintlocks. They fire as one, with devastating aim. The sailor who shot at us rocks as if he's been punched. Three red stains erupt on his shirt as he falls forward, over the gunwale of his boat, into the grey Baltic with a gentle splash. He floats there for a while, face down, bobbing in the swell until his body sinks beneath the waves.

The other Danish sailor, the one who swore at us, is hit twice. He falls dead as well, slumping in a heap into the bottom of his vessel. Both sailors are dead but the Royal Marines are not done their work.

"Throw grenades!" orders Lieutenant Gladding. "Down on deck!"

Tom drops to the decking instantly. "Get down, Duncan!" he shouts. "The Marines mean to sink that boat as well, finish the job proper."

No sooner do I press my body down onto the deck when I hear the sound of clattering metal objects landing onto the deck of the fishing smack, followed within seconds by several loud explosions.

I lift up my head to see smoke and chunks of wood flying up into the air, the smell of gunpowder filling my nose. "Marines stand down!" Gladding barks.

There will be no more firing, no explosions, so I get back to my feet. Tom does as well, though not without a grimace of pain on his face.

"Are ye all right?"

"Back's a little tender still," he explains. "Nothing that won't get better in time, unlike those poor buggers."

I look over our rails to the unfortunate Danish boat rapidly filling with water, sides and bottom holed by the small bombs the Marines tossed, jagged splinters of wood at their edges. The dark northern sea bubbles into the fishing smack. I watch as it fills with water until it swamps, then slips under the surface. A moment later only the tip of the mast and the top of its canvas sail remain, until they too disappear.

"Why did the Cap'n have those men killed?" I ask, as the mast disappears silently into the sea. Save for a few floating pieces of splintered wood, there is nothing left at all to show the boat and the men who sailed it even existed at all.

"He had no choice, Trap. As soon as that fool fired on us his fate was sealed. Firing on a ship of the line? That's an act of war against the Crown. If we don't shoot, then these fellows would have been telling tales at dockside how they raised arms against the Royal Navy and we did nothing in return. Bad for the reputation of the Navy, bad for Cap'n Whitby, bad for us."

"Aye. I suppose I ken why we had to shoot," I say, though

the waste of two lives seems tragic, "but to blow that boat to pieces like that? What was the point?"

"That's easy enough to understand," says Yankee Bill as we sail away. "Ain't no secret that *Cerberus* is sailing in these waters. A thousand sets of eyes or more have seen us since we slipped through the Skagerrak. It's hard to mistake a Royal Navy ship, all black and tan, bristling with cannons with the Jack dancing in the wind."

"If a fishing smack full of dead Danes floats into shore, bodies riddled with musket fire, it wouldn't take no genius to figure out we did it," adds Big Fred. "Provoked or not, that would be a nasty diplomatic incident for London to sort out. Better for everyone if they disappear, lost at sea like. Fewer questions are asked that way."

Chapter 18

I REALIZE WITH a start that I've not thought of my sister for days. Between looking after Tom, completing my duties and worrying about the ever-present danger from the Russians, my mind has been kept occupied, and for a moment I panic when I try to picture what Libby looks like, but can't.

I see her golden hair and the blue of her eyes well enough, but the details of her features begin to escape me. It's only when I think back to that day on the Liverpool docks that her face finally comes fully into view.

My grief at our separation has long been muted. Nearly four years have passed, after all, since we last saw each other. I'm sad to be sure, but the weight of Tom's words has sunk in: "You are both following different stars." Perhaps he is right. It could be that we're not destined to find each other after all.

"Masthead there!" cries the lookout from high in the rigging, shaking me instantly out of my gloom. On the quarterdeck, Lieutenant Murray aims his eyeglass to the north where a large warship, sails furled, and a Royal Navy Jack blowing in the wind has appeared in a bay near the horizon, its black and buff sides contrasting against the grey sky and green trees of the coastline.

She is a ship of the line by the size of her, a massive beast, fifty feet longer than us or more, with two gun decks bristling with cannon.

Captain Whitby appears on the deck, and has been awaiting the sighting, judging by the smile on his face. "Men," he begins when the entire crew stand ready in the waist of the ship, "we are rendezvousing with His Majesty's Ship *Minotaur*. *Prometheus* and *Princess Caroline* will be joining us presently, and the four of us will lay waste to the Russian fleet!"

By now we are only a hundred yards away from *Minotaur*. Her sheer size is staggering. *Minotaur* is a first-rate ship of the line. She dwarfs *Cerberus*, but by the way her crew greets us with huzzahs and cheers, we may well have been the flagship of the fleet.

We respond in kind. We've been at sea now for almost a month, and with the exception of the surly, ill-fated Danish fishermen, have not seen another soul. To encounter fellow sailors from Britain fills our hearts with joy. I never thought in my wildest dreams I would be happy to see more English sailors.

* * *

Within the week the other ships arrive. We make a formidable flotilla. We carry two thousand men and nearly three hundred guns between the four of us. We are invincible, and a jaunty air of confidence sweeps through the crew. "Bring the Russians on!" says Haggis. "The French too! There's naught a navy on earth who can match us!"

"Too right!" says Dutch. "Let Boney 'imself show up! We could end the war in an 'our!"

The bosun's whistle blows sharply. We know what it means, and all hands quickly muster amidships, as a longboat carrying Captain Whitby approaches the port beam. Captain Whitby and the other commanders have been meeting on board *Prometheus*, our flagship, holding a war council.

"Men," says the captain once he climbs the quarterdeck, "we set sail today, to enter the Baltic proper, to sink or capture any Russian ship we find. We will sail as a convoy with ships larger and more heavily armed than us, but by God the *Cerberus* is the best frigate in His Majesty's Royal Navy, and we will show the rest of the fleet how it's done!"

Chapter 19

FOR THE NEXT MONTH we cruise the Baltic, a wolf pack searching for prey. We continue our watches, practise our gunnery and sailsmanship, and polish the brass until it shines, but we never lay eyes on our enemy.

"Damn them! Where can they be?" curses Tom as the sun breaks over the eastern horizon on a rare cloudless day. We are one bell into the morning watch, scouring the horizon from the bow.

As of yesterday Captain Whitby ordered all men to keep their eyes on the sea, to forego swabbing the deck. This deep in enemy waters, keen eyes on the horizon are more important that scrubbed wood. We sail now towards the coast of

Finland, a once independent country, now part of the Russian Empire.

Tensions are high on board *Cerberus*. Our destination is the Archipelago Sea, a shallow, island-studded waterway. The islands are ahead, guarding the gulfs of Finland and Bothnia, the eastern and northern reaches of the Baltic.

"If the Russian Navy is anywhere in the Baltic, it will be in the Archipelago," Lieutenant Wilson told us earlier in the week. "I expect we'll see them bloody soon enough."

He turns out to be right.

Prometheus is several hundred yards off the port while *Princess Caroline* and *Minotaur* cruise on our starboard. As we sail through islands, a patchwork quilt of green in the grey sea, I cannot help noticing the countless bays, narrow straits and inlets.

There are a thousand places or more for the Russian ships to hide out here, and although the sight of the heavily armed warships that cruise alongside us is comforting, I can't help wondering if they will be enough.

"The Russians have the third largest navy on Earth," says Yankee Bill, standing beside Tom and me at the base of the foremast. "There are some 200 enemy ships out here somewhere."

"Two hundred ships to our four." My earlier confidence ebbs when I think of the numbers. "I cannae say I like those odds."

"Aye," agrees Tom. "The Russians are hunting us as much as we them."

But by seven bells of the first watch, and well into the islands, we've seen no Russian sails.

"Set the anchor," commands Lieutenant Murray when we enter a narrow bay.

The last rays of the evening sun have disappeared, leaving only a red and purple glow in the sky. Stars already twinkle overhead through gaps in the cloud. An extra watch is posted to ensure the heavy metal anchor stays fast at the bottom and that we don't drift. Then, at the sound of eight bells, we go below decks to eat.

"Burgoo again tonight, lads," Big Fred says with a big smile, bringing us back our dinner.

"I'm nae terribly fond o' burgoo," I reply, taking my meal, "but at least it's hot."

"Better than the salt beef we've had of late," says Dutch, tucking into the pudding. "After four months at sea the meat's a little off, wouldn't you say?"

He's right at that. The quality of our food has certainly slipped. There's been no butter or cheese for weeks, the biscuits are now thoroughly full of weevils, and salted or not, the pork and beef have started to smell.

"We do have a little surprise for you," says Little Fred, grinning. "We've been saving the grog for the last few days. There's enough to have a proper tipple!"

I don't like the grog any more than I do burgoo. Ship's rum mixed with water and lemon juice is doled out daily. I reluctantly drink the foul-tasting stuff, if only for the lemon juice.

Captain Whitby orders it mixed with the rum to prevent scurvy. Not to drink is insubordination. A look at Tom's back, brutally scarred by the cat, serves as a daily reminder of what happens to a sailor who disobeys orders.

"Another dram, Trap?" says Haggis.

"Nae. I've had my one," but my messmates are not about to let me off so easy.

"As your gun captain I order you to drink, swabbie!" Tom downs his own cup then passes me another. I take the mug and relent.

"You tell 'im, Bull!" says Dutch to the agreement of the rest of the mess.

"A dinnae ken how ye stand the stuff!" I sputter, emptying the cup down my throat.

"With a great deal of practice," replies Yankee Bill, refilling my mug and his own, "and you are in desperate need of some!"

We eat dinner, drink grog, laugh, sing songs and tell stories well into the night. I feel at home with these men, my friends. My family. Tom is right. Like my travels in New Caledonia with Simon Fraser, this has been a tremendous adventure.

After several more mugs of grog, my head swims. My legs, well-practised to walking on a rolling deck, are unable to hold me steady on my feet. "I dinnae feel so well," I say, my stomach suddenly lurching.

"Quick lads," Tom laughs, "help me get Trap above decks before he makes a mess we have to clean up!"

I'm barely aware of what's going on, have only the slightest awareness of my friends helping me through the hatch to the main deck. I lean over the sides, just in time as my stomach heaves, all the burgoo and grog I've swallowed making its way back out. "I reckon I've practised enough fer now," I slur as Tom and the others help me back down below.

Tom lifts me gently into my hammock. "Aye, Trap, you have. Now get some sleep. We'll have plenty more time to practise later."

Chapter 20

"BEAT TO QUARTERS! All hands!" The Royal Marine drums and the sharp sound of the bosun's whistle rouse me from my sleep.

"Smartly now!" cries Gunner Rowe, as I stumble from my hammock, my head pounding, my mouth as dry as the sand that Haggis pours onto the deck around our gun.

Big Fred passes me a mug of water. "Russian sails off the port side. We're in for it now!" Dutch lights the lantern as the ship's boys run to each gun, bringing a tub of water to each, for drinking and putting out fires.

I drain my mug, tuck my hammock away into the netting and stumble towards my station. My stomach heaves again, though after last night, nothing's left in my belly but the rope of spit I cough out onto the wooden floor. I swear to myself I will never drink grog again, no matter how many lashes I get for disobeying the captain's orders.

Tom peers out the gun port at the approaching enemy. "Clever buggers are in gunboats not frigates. Shallow-keeled they are, most likely been hiding in some bay we can't sail into. The Russians waited for us to be at anchor with our sails furled. They have the wind and there's no way we can manoeuvre. We'll just have to wait for 'em to approach, then blow 'em to kingdom come."

Several hundred yards away, low, fast-moving vessels emerge from the shelter of a shallow bay. From their sterns the Russian naval jack, a flag similar to our own Union Jack, blows over the decks, both the sun and the wind at their backs.

The approaching ships are much smaller than *Cerberus*. There are four of them, single-decked, twin-masted yawls each about fifty feet long, a third the length of a frigate, barely a quarter the size of a ship of the line.

The Russians are well-armed. Each small ship has a large cannon facing forward from the bow, with several smaller carronades — short, stubby elevated cannons — as well.

"Damnation!" says Tom. "They don't need to turn sideways to fire when they come in range. Those main guns are 24-pounders by the looks of 'em, enough firepower to sink us. Them carronades will be loaded with grapeshot or chain as well, they mean to kill as many men on the quarterdecks as possible then blast the rigging, to leave us floating helpless like a fish in a barrel."

"Level your guns!" cries Gunner Rowe from somewhere behind me. Haggis and Yankee Bill lift the breech with their handspikes, an action repeated by all the gun crews on the port side. Tom aims at the gunboat sailing towards us then inserts the quoin to level and steady the cannon. My heart races. My task comes next.

"Load with cartridge!" I take the bag of shot from the powder monkey, a young lad named Peter, maybe twelve years of age. Peter's hands shake as he passes me the shot, and his eyes well with tears of fright.

"'Twill be all right," I tell him gently. "When the shooting starts, ye'll be moving too fast to be harmed."

"Thank you, Mr. Trap," the lad says. "I'll make sure I keep you well supplied with shot!"

"Well done," says Tom approvingly. "That lad will cross Hades himself to get us powder now. How are you feeling? Not the best way to wake up, with rum still pounding in your brain."

"Absolutely terrified," I say, tamping the powder and wad down the barrel of the gun. I've forgotten all about my headache and dry mouth. All I can do is focus on the Russian bow.

We strip off our shirts and wrap our kerchiefs around our heads. "It'll get awful hot down here when the guns start blazing," says Yankee Bill, one of only two men in our mess who has seen actual battle.

"Shot and wad your gun!" orders Rowe. Big Fred places the

large iron ball into the mouth of the gun, followed quickly by the cloth wad from Little Fred, both of which I quickly tamp down.

Pudding has assumed the same place he has taken during gunnery practice: behind us, watching every move we make. Today, however, his customary smirk is not on his face. Sweat soaks the front of Midshipman Figg's tunic and he looks as if he's about to cry.

I should, I suppose, find some comfort that he's terrified, but all I can think of is the large cannon on the forward deck of the Russian ship sailing ever closer. "Point your gun!" shouts Rowe.

"It's too small a target!" says a gun captain down towards the bow. "We can't angle our cannon!" Even with the men straining to move their guns with the handspikes, the gunboat that heads directly towards us is narrow. We're built to shoot at large ships that line up sideways against us, not small boats only a dozen feet or so across the beam.

"I said point your guns, blast it all!" shouts Rowe, not prepared to listen to any argument as the approaching Russians loom larger through the gun port. Shots echo across the water as *Prometheus* and our other ships open up their cannon. There is nothing they can do to help us, or us them. It will be every ship for itself.

An enemy ship heads almost directly in a line towards our cannon. For us at least there's no need for any adjustments; we are the only cannon on board that will have a clean shot.

Tom eyes the gunboat carefully as he stares down the barrel of the cannon. "Got him dead to rights. All we need is the order from Master Rowe."

My heart feels as if it will burst from my chest. Any second, Gunner Rowe will command us to fire. Then, the gun deck of *Cerberus* will erupt in noise and smoke, and I will be at war with the Russian Empire.

"Steady lads," says Rowe reassuringly. "Wait for it, wait for . . ." Before he can finish his sentence a large puff of smoke and a distant rumble erupt from the gunboat's large cannon. My mind has barely time to register what I see when the whole world explodes in noise and fire.

A Russian cannonball slams into the side of the ship, tearing through the wooden hull. I'm thrown to the deck with the force of the impact, my ears ringing so loud it feels like church bells are peeling in my brain.

Our guns return fire. The noise is terrible, like thunder, like a hurricane. The deck shakes beneath me, my eyes sting from the smoke, and the acrid odour of the burnt powder envelops my nose.

I try to stand up but a terrible pain erupts in my thigh. I collapse back down to the deck, looking to my leg to see a large jagged splinter, about the size of a belaying pin sticking out of my flesh. My breeches are stained red, with blood pouring out of me onto the deck.

I grab hold of the splinter with both hands, and with sweat dripping in streams off my face, I pull, screaming in agony as the wood slides out of my leg. My stomach heaves, I feel as if I will faint, but know that if I do, I'll bleed to death.

Wood removed, I take the kerchief off my head and wrap it tightly around my leg. It staunches the blood but does little to stop the pain. I am staggering to my feet when another shot smashes into the sides of the ship, knocking me down once more. More splinters fly through the air, though mercifully none hit me this time. Others, however, are not so lucky.

Men, whole or in pieces, lie strewn across the gun deck. Some are alive, though ripped apart by shot and splinters. Their cries are horrific: high-pitched squeals, low agonizing moans and everything in between.

"Help me! For pity's sake, help me!" screams someone through the smoke. Although some of *Cerberus'* cannons still fire, our own is silent. There is no crew left to man it but me.

Haggis is dead. He has taken a direct hit, his body nearly shot in half by the cannonball, his guts pouring out of his stomach, a lake of blood spreading across the deck. I can't see the Freds, Dutch, Yankee Bill or Tom through the smoke, though they must be close by, somewhere.

Then, at the edge of my vision, something moves. I stagger slowly through the smoke to see a shape several feet away. It is Midshipman Figg. Pudding lies slumped over, one hand to his throat, the other flopping like a fish.

A large shard of wood sticks out of his neck, larger by far than the one I pulled from my leg. Blood pours from the wound as Figg tries to say something, but his lips move soundlessly, and I look helplessly down on him until a mass of blood bubbles out of his silent lips, his eyes roll back in their sockets. His arm falls still.

"Trap! Help!" I tear my eyes from Figg, and as the smoke clears, I see Yankee Bill with Tom. Tom is barely conscious by the looks of things, sprawled on the deck. "Bull's hurt! Help me get him to the surgeon!"

I move as quickly as I can. Between the gunfire, the blood on the deck and my leg, it's difficult, but I'm soon standing beside Bill, horrified by what I see. Tom's right leg is nearly shot away. It hangs at an awkward angle above his knee, jagged bone sticking out of the wound.

I wrap the wound with his kerchief, to try to stop the blood that pours out of his leg, but there's nothing the cloth can do to fix the bone.

"Let's get him up," I say. I drape one of Tom's arms over my shoulder, and with Bill doing the same, we start to make our way to the hatch. Doctor Torrance is below on the mess deck, no doubt already busy judging by the scene of carnage around me.

"Leave me be, and fire the gun!" gasps Tom.

"Nae!" I say. "We're taking ye to Doc Torrance! Ye need help or ye'll die!"

But Tom is having none of it. "We'll all die if that big gun hits us again. Blow it out of the sea, Trap. Fire the cannon! Fire now!"

"He's right," says Bill. "We have to do it." The Russian gunboat is almost upon us. We place Tom gently back onto the deck beside the cannon, with Bill wrapping another kerchief around Tom's shattered leg, trying to stem the blood that flows like a river.

The cannon is loaded, primed and ready to go. All that's left for me to do is pull the lanyard and fire. I've seen Tom shoot on several occasions, know what to do, but have never fired it myself. I stare down the barrel, the gunship rising and falling on the waves, now less than one hundred yards away.

"On the down roll," wheezes Tom. "Shoot on the down roll."

I steady my shaking hand, wipe the sweat and grime away from my eyes, and hold tightly onto the lanyard. "One shot, Duncan," he says, his voice is so soft I can hardly hear him. "One good shot is all we need."

I watch as the Russian gun crew tamps down another load of shot, preparing to fire again. Others load their carronades. Any minute now fire and death will fly from their cannon. *Cerberus* is already damaged, goodness knows what a direct hit from this distance will do to us.

"On the down roll." Tom is even quieter this time. "On the down roll." We rise gently on a wave, the cannon aimed at nothing but blue sky until we dip down into the wave's trough, and the bow of the approaching gunboat is all I can see. I brace myself, then pull the lanyard.

I almost forget to move as the gun rolls back, and am nearly mowed down by it. I leap out of the way just in time and before I get back to my feet I hear a great cheer from the deck. I stumble to the gun port to discover by some great miracle I've not only managed to hit the Russians, but I've blown their cannon to pieces.

I must have hit a powder magazine as well; a great cloud of smoke and fire rises up from the gunboat, its crew now in complete disarray. I watch in detached horror as a Russian sailor, completely engulfed in flames, jumps screaming from the deck of his ship into the sea. But I don't care about the Russians. All that's important to me now is taking Tom to Doctor Torrance.

"Bill!" I shout, running over to my friend. "We need to get him to the doctor now!"

Tom looks up to me, his face ashen. His eyes are barely slits, a thin trail of blood runs out from his lips. "There ain't much Doc Torrance can do for me now, Duncan."

"Just hang on, Tom," I cry. "We'll get ye help!"

"Your sister." Tom's voice is now so soft I have to put my ear right to his face. "I was wrong about your stars. When you get back, go find her." Tom's eyes shut for a few seconds, his breath coming in rattled gasps. "Sorry, Duncan. This isn't how I imagined our adventures together endin.'"

"Ye'll be fine," I weep, hugging my friend tightly, knowing it a lie as the words come out of my mouth.

"Bill! Help me lift him!" I cry, but he doesn't move, just looks at me sadly as he stands over Tom's still form. Tom's eyes are open but they don't blink.

His chest is still, no longer rising and falling with the beat of his heart. Even then I frantically pull on Tom's arm, trying to get him to his feet.

"Bill! Will ye not help!"

"I'm so sorry, Trap," Bill says, his own eyes glistening with tears. "Tom's beyond our help now."

Chapter 21

CAPTAIN WHITBY himself says I'm a hero, that I saved *Cerberus*. "And more than that, lad," he says, visiting me as I'm tended by Doctor Torrance. "We won a great victory. *Prometheus* even launched her own ship's boats to counterattack. We destroyed two Russian ships and captured the rest."

I wince as Torrance sticks his curved needle into my leg, drawing another stitch though the skin. "Thank ye, Sir. I'm honoured to have done my duty." But in truth I don't care about my duty, nor do I think I'm a hero. I could have easily missed the Russian gunboat, and ended up dead or shot to pieces like Tom, and so many others.

"You see things in battle that you can't unsee, if you know

what I mean, Trap. Cannon fire can do terrible things to flesh."

Tom told me that. I didn't truly understand what he meant until today, until I saw with my own eyes just what war does to a man. Battle is no grand adventure; it is an abattoir.

The blood of my friends and the choking odour of gunpowder stains my clothes, my hair and my skin. The stink of war has set into my body so deep that bucketloads of sea water are unable to wash it out. I fear the smell will linger in my nostrils forever. And I was the lucky one.

My messmates bore the brunt of the Russian attack. Haggis, Tom, and Big Fred are dead, killed by shot and splinters. They lie piled with the other dead on the main deck. There will be a funeral, similar to that of the migrants who died on the *Sylph* when we travelled to Montreal. There will be a few words about their bravery and sacrifice, then my friends will be tossed overboard, swallowed by the sea. Gone forever.

Those that still live are grievously wounded. Little Fred is blind in one eye from a splinter, and Dutch lost a hand. They are with a score of other injured sailors, fighting for their lives. Only Bill and I escaped relatively unscathed.

"How are you doing?" Bill asks as the needle makes another pass through my leg. "How do you feel?"

How do I feel? I feel grief so deep I can do nothing but stare blankly into space. I feel relief as well that I survived, but it is tainted by a deep guilt that such good men were taken, while I was spared.

How do I feel as I sit here and have my torn leg attended

to while Tom and Haggis and the others lie dead? Mostly I just feel numb.

"Almost done, sailor," says Doctor Torrance. "Half a dozen stitches more and you'll be right as rain."

"Thank ye," I say once more, though his words ring hollow in my ears.

Right as rain.

Doctor Torrance is wrong about that. I'll not be right as rain again for as long as I live.

Chapter 22

"WE'RE GOING HOME, lads," says Captain Whitby three days after the battle. "*Prometheus, Minotaur* and *Princess Caroline* will continue to hunt the Russians, while the *Cerberus* has been tasked with taking the wounded back to England."

Back to England.

I greet the news with a silent prayer of thanks. Finally, I will get to meet Elizabeth Fry and learn what happened to my sister.

The announcement is met with cheers of approval from the rest of the men. *Cerberus* was heavily damaged in the firefight. She has been patched up by the carpenters from wood salvaged from the destroyed Russian ship, but we are in need of greater repair than can be done at sea, in no shape to fight another battle.

"We'll also be escorting our prizes and our prisoners back to London," the captain adds. "The Admiralty will appreciate the additions to the fleet we've provided them."

The men "huzzah" loudly at the remark. The Royal Navy has not become the largest fleet on earth thanks only to our shipyards. Dozens of our ships, from gunboats to ships of the line, have been captured from the Danes, the French, the Russians and any other nation that dares cross us. Several of the Russian ships are still serviceable, and though they pale in size to an English ship of the line, they will make admirable additions to the Royal Navy nevertheless.

As far as the Russian sailors go, experienced seamen are far too dangerous to simply let go. If we dropped them off on an island and left them for their own navy to pick up, they'd be back on a ship within days, threatening British sails.

No, their future involves iron bars, most likely on one of the prison ships floating on the Thames, where they will live and die until peace is restored — if it ever is. Wars have been known to last decades.

"We'll need to reorganize the crew," says Lieutenant Murray. "Half of each watch will be assigned to one of the captured ships to sail them under the command of a midshipman. A Marine contingent will be placed on board each one as well, to guard the prisoners who will be locked up in the holds. Bosun Watson will give you your assignments.

Disperse! Two weeks hard sailing and we'll be at Gravesend!"

I stay aboard *Cerberus*. Though my injury is slight compared to those of some of the men, I'm not fit for my regular duties, so I'm put to work on the quarterdeck, keeping an extra eye for sails. We sail into the wind as the frigate leads the small flotilla back to England, our progress slow as we head through the Baltic, the narrow straits around Amager Island, and back into the Skagerrak.

When we are clear of the straits, I scan the endless ocean, keeping my eyes open for any sign of mast or sail, but see no warships of any navy. In truth I only half-look. My mind swirls. I'd loved life on the ship, being part of the crew. Tom, Haggis and the other lads had become my friends, my companions. My family. But now they are almost all gone. For a while it had been grand. Now? Life on this ship holds no attraction for me anymore.

Libby. I have almost forgotten her, too wrapped up in the adventure of it all to worry about my sister, my real family. I can't believe I was willing to forego her, to cast her aside. I'm ashamed of myself, that it took the deaths of Tom and the others to remember what is truly important. I will find my sister. I must.

* * *

We sail over the top of the Jutland peninsula and enter the slate waters of the North Sea. The wind is now at our back as we bear south. I scan the sea anxiously, looking for the first sign of land. "Penny for your thoughts," says Bill.

"'Tis been four years since my family left Scotland," I tell him as I look to the west. My old home in the Highlands is over there somewhere, far out of view.

"We've both been away a long time, Trap. I've not seen Halifax myself for seven years. I sometimes wonder if I ever will again." A silence descends until Bill asks a cautious question.

"I know you and Bull sailed together before, and that you left a sister behind in Liverpool, but I thought your name was John, but he called you Duncan. I was wondering . . ."

"Aye, my real name is Duncan Scott and my sister's name is Libby." My friends on board have heard snippets of my story, know I left England for Canada, but I've kept much of the details to myself. Until now.

Bill and I have become brothers, bonded by war and the death of our closest friends. If I can't trust him with the truth, who can I? "Our journey began five years ago in Loch Tay, where we were chased off our land," I begin.

"That is quite a tale," he says when I'm done. "So you'll be looking to find your sister when we get back to England, then?"

"Aye. And what will ye do when we're paid out? Ye could go back to Nova Scotia, with some silver in yer pocket." Four days at the most and we will be sailing up the Thames. Our duty to King and country is almost over.

"I've been thinking about that," Bill tells me, "but I ain't sure I'm ready to go home yet."

"Will ye stay in the Royal Navy?"

"I don't think so," he smiles ruefully. "After Tom and the other lads getting killed? I'm starting to think there are better ways to make a living. Who knows? I may stick with you. Searching for your sister seems a lot safer than shooting cannons in the Royal Navy. We've had enough of danger for one lifetime, don't you think?"

Chapter 23

THREE UNEVENTFUL days pass until the cries of "Masthead there!" echo from the lookouts in the fore and mainmasts once more. Captain Whitby hurries out onto the quarter deck, extends his looking glass, staring intently at the sails that have suddenly appeared far to the south.

"Well this is a surprise," he says to Lieutenant Murray, passing him the glass. "It's the *Caledonia*! What the devil is Admiral Pellew doing out here?"

A massive full-rigged ship of the line approaches, sails billowing like clouds. HMS *Caledonia* is monstrous, the Navy's flagship, dwarfing *Minotaur*, *Princess Caroline* and even *Prometheus*. Cannon bristle from three gun decks. A ship that size with that much armament must have a crew of a thousand men or more, I know.

Her very name comes as a surprise as well. I did, after all, spend more than a year in a wild territory thousands of miles away called New Caledonia. *Caledonia* is not alone. Another frigate, almost identical in size to *Cerberus*, floats in the waves beside her. "That's the *Unicorn*," I hear Lieutenant Murray say. "Captain Kerr commands her if I'm not mistaken."

"He does at that," Captain Whitby responds. "I wonder what that old shark is doing out here with the Admiral?"

"We'll soon find out, I wager," says Lieutenant Murray. "It's no accident they are here."

When the ships are two hundred yards apart, *Caledonia* runs up her signal flags. "Blue and yellow checks," says Bill. "Rendezvous. They'll be wanting to talk to the cap'n."

Cerberus launches her ship's boat, both Captain Whitby and Lieutenant Murray aboard. It makes its way to *Caledonia* while we wait anxiously amid decks, our tension rising.

"All hands!" commands Bosun Watson as Captain Whitby and the lieutenant return two hours later, faces set in stone, unreadable.

"Men," the captain says when the entire crew is assembled once more, waiting breathlessly for word. "I know I'd said we were sailing for London, but recent events have forced a change of plans."

"I've a feeling we ain't going back to England quite yet, Trap," whispers Bill. Similar hushed murmurs rise up from the men. Me? I feel numb at the words.

"Avast! Eyes in the boat!" shouts Bosun Watson. At the command, we settle down to await further word. We're one day shy of the Thames estuary. These "recent events" the captain speaks of do not bode well. Judging by the looks on the faces around me, few of the crew are happy, least of all me.

"Admiral Pellew himself has requested our presence on an urgent mission," says Captain Whitby. "While the French fleet has been greatly reduced, they still present a threat to British interests." More hushed talk. There is now little doubt our time on board *Cerberus* will not end anytime soon.

"Three British merchant ships have recently been sunk in the eastern Mediterranean by the French frigates *Incorruptible* and *Revanche*. The Admiralty itself has tasked *Cerberus* and *Unicorn* with finding them."

"Three sunk civilian ships? That hardly seems reason enough to dispatch the flagship of the Royal Navy. Something else is up," says Bill.

"There is more," adds Captain Whitby, as if he heard Bill speak. "These ships carried supplies and food for the island of Malta. As you may know, Malta was freed from occupying French forces nearly ten years ago. Along with Gibraltar, the island is one of our only two territories in possession in the Mediterranean. Napoleon means to take it back, by invasion, starvation or both."

"Sorry, Trap," whispers Bill. "I told you. Looks like you ain't gonna be looking for your sister anytime soon."

"If Malta falls, Napoleon will own the eastern Mediterranean," continues Captain Whitby, as I listen intently. "The

Battle of the Nile, Trafalgar, the uprising in Spain: all our past victories will have been for naught. He will rebuild his naval forces unimpeded, threaten Gibraltar and our armies in the Peninsula, and even perhaps build up enough strength to launch an attack on Great Britain itself."

A hush falls over *Cerberus* as the captain speaks. "*Incorruptible* and *Revanche* are jewels in the crown of Boney's Navy. Forty guns, seven thousand tons, one hundred and fifty feet of warship each. The safety of Malta, our position in the Mediterranean and the existence of the Empire is at stake as long as they sail. We have been tasked by the King himself to capture them if possible, or send them to the bottom if necessary. We will re-provision and make repairs at Gibraltar. Make sail! We are for the Mediterranean and war with Napoleon!"

Chapter 24

CERBERUS' REGULAR crew return from the Russian gunboats, replaced by sailors from *Caledonia*. Our wounded are taken aboard the flagship, several dozen kegs of beer, rum, water and beef are loaded into our hold, food and drink enough to last until Gibraltar, and when we are ready, the helmsman adjusts our course.

Instead of turning due west into the Thames, we are now heading southwest through the English Channel, *Unicorn* off our port bow, skirting the coastline of Kent and East Sussex.

"What's that o'er there?" I ask Bill as a long line of white rises above the distant English shore. We are on deck, Bill, Little Fred and I, waiting for our watch to begin. I can't think of a time I felt more defeated and am trying to forget about my dashed hopes.

"Dover. The White Cliffs. They're a landmark of sorts, for sailors coming home — and leaving it. I wonder if we'll ever see them again. Russian gunboats are one thing. The French are something else entirely."

"*If* we ever see them again," I say. "Why does it seem that whenever the blasted British Empire has a problem I'm sent to help fix it?"

"Come now, Trap," encourages Bill. "Stiff upper lip as the proper gentlemen say. 'Tis only two ships we're hunting. Surely *Cerberus* is equal to the task."

"Mayhaps. Mayhaps not." Little Fred sombrely adjusts the newly acquired patch over the empty socket where his left eye used to be. Injured or not, neither he nor I have wounds serious enough to be excused from active duty. "Let's not forget the French didn't become masters of Europe without knowing how to win battles at land — and sea."

"No doubt Boney's been knocked about," says Bill, "but the French fleet ain't no pushover. Besides, I wouldn't be surprised if there's more than two frigates waiting for us off the coast of Sicily or wherever else we're sailing."

We make our way south, past the coasts of France and Spain. As we sail, the weather warms, and the sun beats down harshly onto the deck of the ship and the backs of the men.

In response, most of us have taken to going shirtless on duty and off, thick clothes we wore in the cold waters of the

Baltic tucked away in our chests. Our skin browns, glowing with a constant sheen of sweat.

Below decks the air is stuffy, the heat insufferable. We sleep in the open air, in corners of the deck where we won't get in the way of the duty watch.

Bill, Little Fred and I have been reassigned. We are still responsible for a gun, but we now fire one of the 24-pound carronades on the forecastle, on the open deck in front of the foremast.

The carronade is usually manned by the best gunners. Captain Whitby apparently counts us amongst that number for the work we did to sink the Russian ship. We have a new member of our gun crew as well.

Young Peter, the powder monkey who fetched us shot back in the Baltic, has been promoted to sponger on our gun crew. He is but a lad, barely into his teens, but in the eyes of the Royal Navy he is a man and a sailor.

"The carronade is a nasty piece of work, lads," says Gunner Rowe as he trains us on the new weapon. "Easy to move up and down, and pivot left to right. You'll be gun captain, Trap," he tells me. "Your mates will help load and sponge."

"Aye, Gunner," I say.

"A sharpshooter like you will put it to maximum effect," Rowe adds. "The carronade fires balls like the guns below, but when we meet the French you'll be firing grapeshot and chains into the sails, the rigging and the bodies of anyone unfortunate enough to be in your line of fire."

* * *

"That's Portugal you see, lads," says Lieutenant Wilson as a rocky brown coastline appears to the east a week later. We've sailed through the rough waters of the Bay of Biscay and now speed our way south, almost out into the wide open Atlantic.

"As we speak, the British Army is meeting the French on the field somewhere over there. I'd not give up the sea for almost anything, but to fight alongside General Wellesley? That would be a remarkable experience."

"Sir, who's General Wellesley?" I ask.

"Wellesley's the commander of British forces on the Peninsula," Wilson says. "He's an absolute genius at war. The Royal Navy can keep Napoleon at bay for years, but to truly defeat him, the Army will have to win on land, and there's no better man to lead our forces to victory than Wellesley."

Fortunately, the land war is not our concern. And once we clear Cape St. Vincent, the southern tip of Portugal, we turn due east to enter the Mediterranean, with worried thoughts of French warships occupying our minds.

The mood on board is mixed. The professional sailors take the new target in stride. War is their job — they sail to wherever the fight is and will do their duty with grim determination. Some even cheer the thought of going after Napoleon's ships.

Most of the pressed men, myself amongst them, however, are angry at the change of plans. The Baltic had been a short campaign, and many of us looked forward to ending our service. We all have our reasons to want off *Cerberus*. I don't know how quite yet, but I will leave this ship anyway I can and make my way back to England.

These thoughts swirl through my head as we continue east. "The Pillars of Hercules," says Bill, as two large mountains appear in the distance, one on either side of the strait. "The Rock of Gibraltar to the north and Jebel Musa to the south. They mark the entrance of the Mediterranean. Africa and Europe, separated by less than eight miles."

The Pillars of Hercules.

It is easy to see why the large stone crags have earned that name. As we sail through the Strait of Gibraltar, I can easily imagine that ancient hero, perched either foot on top of them, surveying the world from up high.

The sails flutter for a moment as *Cerberus* changes direction, now sailing towards the Rock of Gibraltar. Within a few hours we enter the port. The day has been fiercely hot, and we are grateful when the sun dips behind the Rock and for the cooling wind that blows off the sea.

Cerberus and *Unicorn* tie up alongside a long breakwater in the harbour. Above us, creeping up the brown hills, are a patchwork tangle of stone houses, packed tightly together on narrow streets. The harbour itself is just as crowded.

At least three other frigates, one ship of the line and any number of smaller vessels, all flying the Union Jack, are berthed along the docks or at anchor in the harbour.

"Right lads," says Bosun Watson, once the victualling crew

has been assembled. Fresh food and grog is on the dock. "Load 'em up and stow 'em below."

Empty kegs that once held water, pickled beef, beer and any number of other foodstuffs are quickly replaced by heavy sealed-oak casks full of the food, water and beer that will sustain us as we prowl the Mediterranean, seeking out the French vessels audacious enough to seize English merchant ships.

"Trap! Get dockside and help those swabbies out!" says Watson after a barrel nearly slides out of the netting into the dirty water of the port. "The food's bad enough in the Navy without letting it take a swim in the sea."

"Aye, bosun." I walk gingerly down the gangplank. For the last three months I've been at sea, my legs have been accustomed to the swaying of the deck below me. To move about on wood that doesn't rock below me is unsettling, and I nearly fall several times.

"Avast!" laughs Watson, to the merriment of the crew. "Get your legs beneath you and see to the barrels! What kind of marksman can't handle a little stroll portside?"

I help the stevedores load the kegs and crates into the nets as the crew on *Cerberus* hauls them up with the davits, then carries them below decks.

Within two hours we are resupplied, then the ship is turned over to the carpenters. Soon the entire side of *Cerberus* swarms with men swinging hammers and wielding saws. I watch them work until the whistle blows for dinner.

We've eaten nothing but wormy and rancid food for the last months and I'm eager to have a dinner of fresh beef and biscuits, untouched by the weevils.

"How long do ye think we'll be in port?" I ask Bill.

"As short a time as possible, I hope. I hate this damnable hot weather. I'd rather fight the entire French fleet than spend another night in this oven!"

Chapter 25

YANKEE BILL GETS his wish four days later. Fully victualled, and with the dockyard carpenters completing the repairs, we slip out onto the still waters of Gibraltar harbour, though we are two crewmen lighter.

Two pressed men from the port watch who'd come aboard with me at Deptford have disappeared, vanishing sometime in the night. I had considered it myself, was even asked to join them, but Bill, like Tom when we sailed from London, counselled me out of it.

"I'm glad you listened to reason and stayed aboard," says Bill, after we've searched the ship fruitlessly from the bilge to the masts for the missing men. "It's death to desert ship here. Gibraltar's a pinprick of land, crawling with British sailors, soldiers and Royal Marines."

"What do ye mean?" I ask. "I thought pressed men weren't executed fer leaving the ship?"

"Not by the Royal Navy they ain't," Bill says. "A few lashes and its back on board, but a far worse fate is waiting for those who try to escape the Rock overland. They'd die of thirst, get picked up by the Spanish as spies or captured by the French and shot. Life on *Cerberus* ain't grand, but believe me, Trap, there are far worse captains to sail for than Captain Whitby."

I take Bill at his word. Many of the crew have sailed on different ships, both navy and merchant. They have both tales and the scars of the cat to vouch for the cruelty of their former captains.

"Eyes on the sea at all times," says Lieutenant Wilson as Gibraltar disappears from sight behind us. "The French could be anywhere. This close to Africa, Barbary Corsairs plague these waters, too. They'd love to catch a frigate like us unawares, and I'd prefer not to end up in the slave markets of Tunis if I can help it."

"Who are the Corsairs, Sir?"

"Pirates from the North African coast, Stuart," Wilson says grimly. "Arabs for the most part, but more than a few Europeans sail in their ranks, seizing merchant ships then selling their crews into slavery. Worse than the French, the

Corsairs are. I hope we see one. I'd like nothing better than to send them to Davy Jones' locker."

* * *

Two days out of Gibraltar, the Mediterranean belongs to *Cerberus* and *Unicorn*. We sail northeast right in the middle of the sea, far from both the European and African coast. We see no French warships or pirate vessels, nor do we lay eyes on any of the coast-clinging fishing and transport ships that ply the waters closer to shore. We are alone on the green sea, scudding towards Sicily and the last known location of the French frigates.

Even with the wind, the heat is oppressive, as hot or hotter as it ever was in the desert wastelands above Fraser's River, but at least we have an ample supply of water stored in the kegs below decks. I know how horribly thirst can burn the throat of a traveller who has run dry.

Most of the crew wear nothing but our linen breeches and kerchiefs tied around either our necks or foreheads. Shoes have long been put aside, and we are all burned nut-brown by the sun.

By mid-afternoon of our third day from Gibraltar, however, the temperature drops, the skies overhead darken and the wind slackens. It is an ominous sign, one I recognize from my trip across the Atlantic.

Bosun Watson eyes the rapidly blackening sky as well. "Storm coming, Sir."

"Indeed it is," says Lieutenant Wilson. "Make ready the ship."

"All hands! Reef the sails!" commands the bosun. "Batten hatches and secure the deck. Smartly now, lads! Weather's fast approaching. Boney can wait for us to ride the gale out."

The topmen quickly scramble up the masts to pull in canvas. The wind is coming directly behind us, and only a few sails are needed to keep us moving and on course.

"Grab a hammer, Trap," says Bill, as he takes a handful of tarpaulins, nails and wooden slats from a chest on the deck. The hatches that lead to the gun decks are covered with a latticed hatch. In rough seas or when the rain falls heavily, our job is to cover the hatches with the tarps then nail them down with the wooden battens to hold them in place.

"Nervous?" Bill asks me as we go about our work.

"Aye." I know first-hand the damage a storm can cause. I think back to the *Sylph*, to hours spent on the pump, trying desperately to keep the ship afloat. I remember poor old Francis, crushed by a falling spar, his body swept overboard.

I saved Tom's life that day. He had been caught in the webbing, dangling over the black Atlantic. My hand the only thing keeping him alive. Who could have known that day that we would sail together again, Tom and I, or that he would die on board *Cerberus*, fighting the Russians in service to his country.

There is little time to waste on these sad memories, however. The storm is quickly upon us. It seems not as rough as the gale that engulfed the *Sylph*. I'm not sure if that's because the storm is smaller or that *Cerberus* is a larger ship, able to better withstand the wave and wind that slam into our sides, tossing us about like a cork on the water.

On the quarterdeck, Captain Whitby, Lieutenant Murray and Second Lieutenant Wilson stand beside the helmsman. Captain Whitby issues commands with a quiet confidence, seemingly unfazed by the tempest. This is the Royal Navy after all, and routines are carried on, regardless of the weather.

Dressed in waterproof oilers, we take our turns on watch, manning the bilge pumps, replacing tarpaulins that blow off the hatches, and keeping our eyes on the rigging, the sails and the horizon, alert for any shredded canvas or broken line.

When we are not on watch, we try our best to catch some snatches of sleep, though rest is almost impossible with the water streaming through gaps in the decking and our hammocks rocking violently with every roll.

When we don't sleep we stick to our regular tasks, including eating. With the storm, however, the cook has extinguished the fire, and serves us cold beef and biscuits, though most of us — including me — are too sick to eat much at all.

"Masthead there! Off the starboard bow!" cries a lookout at dusk on the second day of the storm. He is scarcely heard above the wind that howls through the sheets and rigging, or the peals of thunder that ring across the black sky, illuminated by forks of crackling lighting.

"Beat to quarters!" cries Bosun Watson as Bill and I make our way to the carronade. Below decks the gun crews will be scurrying to their cannons, preparing to rain iron and death upon whoever sails ahead of us, should the order be given.

"How on earth are we to fire a gun in this weather?" I ask. The rain is coming down in sheets, and the deck heaves up and down, left to right, with every wave. "A dinnae ken if I could aim a pistol in this storm, let alone a ship's cannon."

"Hopefully we won't have to, Trap," Bill says. "It's hard enough fighting the weather. Let's pray it's a fishing vessel."

Captain Whitby has his glass pressed firmly to his eye, trying to make out the nature of the distant sails that appear and disappear with every roll of the waves. "What do you see, Sir?" asks Second Lieutenant Wilson.

"Frigate by the looks of it," Whitby replies. "I'd stake my life on it."

"The *Unicorn*?" Since the storm began, we have been blown away from our sister ship and have lost sight of her.

"I don't think so." Whitby's eyeglass still trains on the distant ship. "Lines are wrong, sails are wrong. Whoever she is, that ship isn't one of ours."

"Algerians, perhaps?" says Murray. "Look to the stern. Do you see a red triangle? It could be the *Mashouda*, the Barbary flagship. Do we go after it? These damned pirates have been plaguing these waters for years. This could be our chance to strike a blow at the very heart of the Barbary Coast itself!"

"There's a flag all right," says Captain Whitby grimly,

lowering the glass. "White with a red, white and blue canton in the corner. Not pirates, French for sure, and we're gaining on her!"

"Incorruptible or *Revanche?"* Not that it matters to Lieutenant Murray by the excitement in his voice. Nor does he care how fiercely the wind blows. He is a warrior and a patriot. He would follow the French into a hurricane if it meant striking a blow at the heart of Napoleon Bonaparte's Navy.

"I can't read the name, Sir," Second Lieutenant Wilson tells him, "but one of them for sure. Do we engage? In this weather? Sink or capture, the orders were. A French frigate would make a fine prize, but the seas are too rough to board her. We'd have to send her to the bottom."

Wilson is as eager to carry out his duty as Lieutenant Murray, but he serves as the cautious voice of reason on *Cerberus.*

"Aye," says Captain Whitby. "We engage and we will blow her to pieces. Goodness knows how many better chances we'll have. Prepare for battle."

Whitby's orders echo across the ship. "Don't forget Nelson's words at Trafalgar: 'England expects that every man will do his duty.' Weather be damned, we will do ours! To battle, men! I want that ship resting on the bottom of the sea before morning!"

Chapter 26

THE HUNT FOR the French frigate is like nothing I have ever experienced. What little light that comes from the cloud-covered dusk sky is soon conquered by night and the storm. Captain Whitby has ordered our ship's lights extinguished, as has the master of the French ship. We hunt in darkness, our prey visible only when lightning erupts from the sky.

"Where the blazes is she?" Bill asks. We stand ready on the bow, wind, waves and rain pelting us, carronade prepared to fire upon the French. Below us on the gun deck, Gunner Rowe has all twenty-six of our 18-pounders ready to fire from either side of the ship.

"A dinnae ken, Bill. She was last seen off the starboard

bow but the ship could be anywhere now, port or starboard, bow or stern. 'Tis like trying to find a lump of coal at midnight," I reply. We've not laid eyes on the enemy frigate for more than an hour. She could be anywhere.

Suddenly thunder erupts right over our head, louder than a thousand church bells, or the largest cannon on earth. "Damn them all to hell!" cries Bill as jagged forks of lighting turn night to day. "There she is!"

We have pulled even with the French. Not two hundred yards starboard they ride the crest of a massive wave, their side lined up to ours, in perfect firing position.

"Fire!" cries Captain Whitby. The French captain issues the same order, and I watch transfixed as the sea in front of me erupts in fire and smoke, the roar of French and English guns shaking *Cerberus* from stem to stern.

"Shoot, Trap!" shouts Bill. Our carronade is shot and wadded, and by good planning as much as luck is aimed directly at the French midships. The carronade fires all manner of things: cannonballs, chainshot and grapeshot.

Gunner Rowe has instructed us to load chainshot, two balls connected by a long length of chain — a nasty charge meant to rip masts, sails and sailors to shreds. I pull the lanyard and the hammer falls onto the dry powder.

Cerberus shudders with the force of our cannon. The deck shakes once, every inch of my body ringing with noise.

From this range, on calm seas, the two broadsides would have devastating effect. Spars and men's limbs should be shattered. Sails should be holed. Jagged holes should be ripped into the oaken sides of the ship. On the gun decks men should be lying dead or screaming as legs and guts are blown away.

That does not happen. The seas are wild as we open fire on each other. Instead of taking a direct hit, *Cerberus* lunges madly up onto the crest of a wave at the same time the French frigate plunges deep into a trench. Our cannon shot flies harmlessly into the empty air above the French while theirs hits the water far under our keel.

"Swab and sponge!" I cry to Little Fred and young Peter. "Are ye all right?" I ask our youngest gunner, his eyes wide, his hands shaking as he sponges the carronade.

"I'm too scared to breathe," Peter says, his voice shaking.

"I don't care if you breathe," Little Fred tells him. "Just sponge the gun and be quick about it!"

"Fire!" cries Captain Whitby just as we finish reloading. This time when I pull the lanyard we fire completely blind. The sky is black, the air on deck full of rain and smoke, the French frigate nowhere to be seen.

"Do ye see them?" The smoke clears from my eyes as Bill, Little Fred and Peter reload the carronade once more. Before the words leave my mouth there is the flash of cannon fire. It is further away, at least 800 yards now; still within range of the large guns below, but too far for the short-barrelled carronade.

The deck erupts in smoke and flame once more as we

return fire. I can't see whether any of our balls strike home, but this time a French shot comes closer. Even with the waves I see the splash of a cannonball hitting the water just off our stern.

"Hold your fire!" orders Captain Whitby as the French disappear into the storm and the darkness once more.

All eyes are trained on the sea, searching everywhere for the French. "There she is!" I cry a few minutes later as lightning flashes overhead. Somehow I manage to catch just a fleeting glimpse of the enemy frigate. It is 2,000 yards away now, drifting away in the waves. To fire now would be a waste of lead and powder.

"Damnation!" Lieutenant Murray curses. "If it wasn't for this cursed storm we'd have had them."

"Perhaps," says Captain Whitby, "but now at least one of Boney's captains know we're after them. They can run, Lieutenant Murray, but they cannot hide forever. There are ten thousand bays and harbours in the Mediterranean, and if we have to search every one until we find them, then by God that is what we will do. The French may have escaped us this time, but they will not do it again."

Chapter 27

BY MORNING THE storm blows itself out. The sky clears, and the sun shines bright and hot, reflecting on the azure surface of the Mediterranean like diamonds. I walk the deck of *Cerberus* alone, lost in my thoughts.

Battle or not, I am desperate to find a way to slip from *Cerberus* and make my way back to England, but for now I must focus on my duties. We are on a war footing; we drill with the guns daily, even firing live shot, and for the first time we are trained on the cutlass.

"Form single ranks, four feet apart!" orders Lieutenant Gladding, commanding officer of the Royal Marine detachment. We line up bare-chested on the main deck. The sun is still low on the horizon, the day only a few hours old, but it is hot, and we are already sweating.

"Don't cut yourselves, you tars," says Gladding as we each take a short, curved sword from the gunner's mate. "You're not about to become Knights of the Round Table, but with a bit of luck you'll learn enough to use a cutlass without killing yourselves."

I hold the cutlass in my clammy hand. It's heavier than I would have imagined. Much more so than any knife I've used, and deadlier by far.

"Right," Gladding says, lifting his own weapon. "We've not the time to teach you everything, so we'll start with the basics. Swords up! Time you learned the *moulinet*."

An hour later I feel as if my arm will fall from my shoulder. Gladding, in his full uniform, has hardly a glow on his forehead, while all of us sailors are soaked.

There is no fighting. All we have done is move the sword in circular motions, to the left and the right, over and over.

"That's it, tars," he finally says. "First lesson is over. Hand in the swords to the gunner's mate."

"Och! I'll never be able to use my arm again!" I groan, collapsing in a heap onto the deck. My entire arm from my fingers to shoulder feels as if it's on fire.

"Give me knife or a pistol any day," says Bill. He lies on the deck beside me, rubbing his aching wrist. "I hate to say it, but the Marines have gone up a little in my estimation! I never want to hold a blasted cutlass again!"

Cutlass lessons continue the next morning, however, the one after that and every morning for the rest of the week. Gladding drills us mercilessly, teaching us the art of sword-play. We practise the *moulinet* over and over until he's satisfied, then moves on, one step at a time, teaching us how to defend ourselves from a blow, then to go on the offensive.

"Cut, thrust, parry, feint. With a few hundred hours of practice some of you might make decent swordsmen," Gladding says approvingly seven days later. "At the very least, you've given yourselves a sporting chance not to get gutted if you end up fighting the French hand-to-hand."

* * *

Another week passes. By now we are deep into the Mediterranean and the brown mountains of Sicily have appeared in the distance, rising above the green water of the sea.

We have reunited with the *Unicorn* as well. Captains Kerr and Whitby had anticipated a separation on the journey to Sicily and had arranged to rendezvous in a sheltered bay on the southern tip of Marettimo, a small island off the western coast of Sicily.

Together again we patrol the coastline, seeking out the French frigates. Ships and smaller vessels sail everywhere: small coastal fishing boats and a host of other strange-looking vessels with sleek hulls, large, triangular sails, and strange, musical names like *Xebec, Mistoco, Trabacollo* and *Felucca*.

We have stopped several of them, asking their captains if they have seen the French ships, but as the days go by the answer remains the same. No sign of the French, not even a whisper. Napoleon's frigates remain ghosts, but we do see other dangerous things in the water.

"Look to the sea, Trap," says Bill as we stand on deck, searching the sea for sails.

After all this time at sea I am used to dolphins. They frequently swim beside us, dancing and playing in the wake or alongside the bow as it cuts through the water. The grey, triangular fins I see now belong to no dolphin.

"Sharks, the real wolves of the sea. Not a good time to go for a swim." This is the first time we have seen sharks on our travels, and the old sailors take it as a dark omen.

"Some say sharks can smell blood in the water a mile away," Little Fred says. "They are a portent of death. Battle's coming soon enough; the sharks are waiting around for a meal."

Cerberus and *Unicorn* are in a constant state of readiness. Gun hatches are open, cannons at the ready, all set to blast the enemy to blazes. None of the vessels we see, however, fly the flag of France.

We sail along the southern coast of Sicily when, in the late evening three days after seeing the sharks and with just one bell left in the second dog watch, sails suddenly appear.

They look like white billowing clouds as they emerge out of a hidden Sicilian bay far up the coastline. The familiar cry of "masthead there!" rings out across the ship as we move to the sound of the drum and the cry of "beat to quarters!"

"Most likely a fisherman leaving port," says Bill as we stand by the carronade, our cutlasses standing ready in racks beside the mast. We are on a war footing, and Lieutenant Gladding has seen fit to keep us armed.

"Aye, most likely." This is the tenth time at least we've drummed to stations since seeing Sicily. We are well practised, ready to engage our enemy with broadsides and sword, but have yet to find them.

"Hold on, I may have spoken too soon, Trap." Bill eyes the far-off ship keenly. "That's no fishing schooner; she's a frigate, full-rigged for sure, with gun ports. Whatever she is, she belongs to someone's navy. Stand ready."

On the quarterdeck, Captain Whitby, Lieutenant Murray and Lieutenant Wilson have their glasses pressed to their eyes. One by one they lower the long brass telescopes, the grim looks on their faces confirming that they've come to the same conclusion as Bill.

"French frigate! Two points off the starboard bow!" cries Murray. "Battle stations!"

Hearts race as we leap into action. I spread sand around our gun, knowing now from personal experience how slippery the wooden deck of a ship can be when it's covered with blood.

"Ye'll be fine, Peter," I say to the youngest member of our gun crew. Just a few short months ago the lad was a powder monkey, running bags of gunpowder between the magazines and the guns. Now, he is an experienced sponger. Bill will load the shot and help aim the carronade, while I fire.

Gunner Rowe has armed us with lead canisters of small grapeshot, as well as chainshot. Our task will be to shred the sails, the lines and the men on the main deck.

The distance between *Unicorn*, *Cerberus* and the French frigate closes. A large white banner with a red, white and blue canton in the corner flies proudly in the wind. Though it is too far away to see with the naked eye, Captain Whitby can make out her name through his spyglass.

"The *Incorruptible*. Forty-four guns by the looks of it. There are two against one. We have more sail and we are upwind; we have the weather gauge. She can't outrun us, and her captain knows it. Make sure the men are ready, lieutenants; we'll be at war within the hour!"

"A bit bigger than a Russian gunboat, eh, Trap?" says Bill as the distance between us evaporates. The wind blows briskly at our back, as *Unicorn* and *Cerberus* fairly race through the waves towards the French frigate.

"Aye. A bit bigger, indeed." Staring at the approaching French warship, I begin to tremble. *Incorruptible* is bigger than us, longer, heavier, and with more guns. The *Unicorn* and the weather gauge or not, we are in for the fight of our lives.

"She's trapped. Ain't nowhere to go," says Bosun Watson. "Land to the back of her, Royal Navy to the front. Weren't expecting us to show up like this, I reckon. She's caught with her breeches down, so to speak. All the French can do is swing around, fire broadsides and fight like the devil."

Below us on the gun deck, Gunner Rowe is preparing the cannon and crew, ensuring all is in readiness, waiting for Captain Whitby to close the distance, order the ship to come about swiftly and give him the order to fire.

The plan is simple. *Cerberus* will slide through the water, present her starboard side to the French while *Unicorn* swings to the port. Twenty-six guns will fire at the same time, unleashing massive broadsides. The French will do the same and while it is two ships to one, they will have twenty cannon of their own, and will not surrender without the fight of their lives.

On the main deck, preparations of an equally deadly but much different sort are being made. The Marine sharp-shooters have climbed into the rigging to the fighting tops.

With their long flintlocks they will take aim at *Incorruptible*'s exposed gunners and officers, killing as many as they can — as well as the French Marines in their own fighting tops, who aim to kill our officers and crew.

When the two ships come together, the Marines will take the lead, boarding the French as they toss grenades onto the French deck before leading the men onto the French ship itself, fighting at close quarters with cutlass and pistol.

"Your job is simple enough, lads," says Second Lieutenant Wilson to Bill and me. "We'll be going in bow-first until the last moment when the helmsman comes about. Before he does, you'll aim the carronade dead ahead, fire on my command, and rake the men on the deck, the rigging and the sails. You'll cause as much damage as you can with your chainshot, then you'll reposition your gun when we turn and keep firing until the gun barrel melts, you're given the order to stop, or you're dead!"

The drums roll. We are hurriedly beaten to quarters, not ten minutes before we engage the French in battle. "Men of England," says Captain Whitby to the assembled crew, "we are about to fight a warship from Napoleon's fleet, the greatest enemy to the security of our people since the Spanish Armada, more than two hundred years ago."

I stand breathless, excitement and fear coursing through my veins. "The Royal Navy is the only thing that stands between our shores and invasion," he continues. "King George and the people of England are counting on you to do your duty, and by God you will not let them down. Capture her if you can, sink her if you must, but before the sun sets, *Incorruptible* will be ours!"

Chapter 28

"FIRE!" CRIES LIEUTENANT WILSON when the French warship comes into range. I take a deep breath, pull the lanyard, then step quickly out of the way as the carronade bounces backward as it sends its deadly load of chainshot towards *Incorruptible*.

"Well done, Trap!" cries Bill, although I can scarcely hear him through the ringing in my ears. Our first shot has found its mark in the sails of the foremast.

I've managed to shred a sail and send chunks of spar splintering down onto the French deck. I watch as sailors run for cover, desperately trying to avoid the falling wood.

We don't have time to congratulate ourselves. Peter quickly

sponges out the gun, and Bill reloads, this time with a nasty-looking grapeshot. I fire again, this time onto the deck of the ship itself, right towards the crew.

We are close enough to hear the French sailors scream. The shot tears across *Incorruptible*'s wooden deck. I can't see for certain through the smoke what damage we've inflicted, but I've no doubt more than a handful of our enemy have been separated from their limbs or their lives. I also know that their deck runs thick with blood because my aim was true.

I have just killed people, men and boys alike, my own age or younger. I suppose that later those screams and the rest of what I see and hear today will haunt me, but I have no time to dwell on that now.

A plume of smoke and the sound of thunder erupts from the carronade on the bow of *Incorruptible*. The French have mounted their counterattack, sending their own grapeshot our way.

I throw myself to the deck as hundreds of the tiny balls fly through the air above me, slamming into the foremast, ripping through our sails like deadly hailstones.

A Marine in the fighting top cries out, then tumbles from the mast headfirst, landing with a heavy thud onto the deck just behind me. He lies still on the deck, limbs and neck twisted in strange angles, blood pouring out of the large hole in his belly.

Incorruptible starts to turn, preparing to unleash her main cannons. "Keep firing!" commands Lieutenant Wilson. I feel dizzy, overwhelmed by the smell of the gunpowder, the noise of the gun, and the taste of sweat in my mouth. Bill loads the carronade again. I pull the lanyard, then send another load of iron into French men and sails. More screams. More blood.

"Come about!" shouts Lieutenant Wilson. The helmsman turns the ship's wheel sharply and *Cerberus* heels over, her stern sliding through the water. The frigates are now less than two hundred yards apart.

Even before *Cerberus* is fully sideways, the guns below me open up. All thirteen of the starboard guns fire as one. The ship shakes from the force of them, and I watch in dreadful awe as the wooden sides of *Incorruptible* splinter as our shots pound into her. *Unicorn* does the same. From the deck it seems as if all the cannonballs strike home.

The setting sun bathes us in a red glow. With the clouds of smoke obscuring the ships, the flashes of flame flaring out of the guns and the cries of wounded and dying men, there is something demonic about this battle, as if we are in hell itself. On the shore I see the lights of a small town, and I cannot help wondering what we must look like to the civilians onshore.

A French cannonball smashes into our quarterdeck. The force of shot throws us both to the deck. We are unharmed, but when we stagger to our feet we soon learn that we are more fortunate than some.

The helmsman, Captain Whitby and Lieutenant Murray still live, though Murray has a long splinter sticking out of his forearm. Second Lieutenant Wilson, however, is not so fortunate. He has been hit by a full load of shot. What's left of the commander of the starboard watch lies spread around the quarterdeck in bloodied pieces large and small.

"Back to your stations!" orders Captain Whitby, climbing to his feet, wiping a stream of blood away from his face. Murray grasps the wood stuck in his arm and pulls it out with a grunt. He ties off the wound with his kerchief and takes his place beside the captain, as if the splinter was nothing more than a mosquito bite.

I tear my eyes from the carnage on the quarterdeck as Bill, Peter and I heave on the carronade, repositioning it.

Once our carronade is aimed at *Incorruptible* I fire, sending chainshot into the French rigging. For the third time since the battle began, shattered wood and rope fall to the deck of the French ship and sailors scream out in agony. I ignore them and fire again and again, as *Cerberus* and *Incorruptible* drift closer and closer to each other.

Suddenly, the large guns below fall silent. "Why aren't they shooting?" I ask Bill, wiping the sweat and gunpowder from my face.

"We're too close to each other. The French have stopped firing, too. If either one of us hits each other's powder magazine we'll both be blown to smithereens. We're in between *Unicorn* and the French as well, so she can't fire either. From here on out it's side arms and cutlasses. We'll be boarding her any minute now."

We are now only fifty yards or so from the French. The sun is gone and *Incorruptible* looms in silhouette in the twilight, so close I could almost reach out and touch her.

"Boarding party ready!" cries Lieutenant Gladding. The Royal Marines form up beside him, pistols and swords at the ready.

The only shooting now comes from the snipers in the fighting tops in both ships. Musket balls whiz through the air, thudding into wood — and frequently into flesh. These guns are smaller than cannon, but just as deadly.

Barely twenty yards separates the two warships. "Prepare grappling hooks!" Gladding commands. A dozen sailors line up on the side, sharp anchor-like hooks attached to lengths of rope in their hands.

"As we come together the Marines will throw those hooks into the lower rigging and swing aboard," says Bill. "We'll follow with our cutlasses when the decks collide."

I can barely breathe. My sword shakes in my hand as I hear shouting and cheers in French and English as the crews prepare to slaughter each other. I've killed only one man at such close quarters: La Malice, in self-defence on the banks of Fraser's River in what seems a lifetime ago.

I've never been able to get that memory from my head, had hoped never to have to do such a thing again, but here I stand, sword in my shaking hand ready to kill or be killed.

Without warning, a small metal object bounces on the deck before me. It is the size of a large apple, with a smoking fuse sticking out its side. "Jump!" cries Bill. My friend takes my arm, pulling me away from the grenade as it goes off.

Shrapnel flies through the air, whizzing past me like angry wasps. The force of the blast throws me off my feet, lifting me to the side of the ship. I bounce into the wooden rail then over it. Before I can even take a breath, I hit the water and disappear under the surface.

I'm deep in the blackening water when I come to my senses. I panic as I look through the water above me. I see fire, hear the muzzled sound of shots. I kick furiously towards the surface, my lungs burning for want of air. I feel as if it's too far, that I won't make it, then my head bursts free. I gasp, cough and sputter as I breathe once more.

"For goodness sake be quiet!" hisses Yankee Bill. He's holding onto a piece of flotsam, a chunk of thick broken spar from one ship or the other, his head barely above the water, a grimace of pain on his face.

"Are ye all right?" I whisper.

"I dunno," he says. "My left leg feels as if it's burning, and I can't feel my foot. What about you?"

Through some miracle I have avoided serious injury. My ears ring, though whether from the cannon fire or grenade I can't tell. I have a cut on my shoulder from a piece of shrapnel, no doubt, and my left side hurts from hitting the rails before I fell overboard, but that seems to be the extent of my wounds.

The water around us is red, both because of the reflection of the fires but also from blood that swirls around us in the water. I fear it comes from my friend's leg. "Can ye lift yer leg?" I ask.

With a grunt of pain, Bill does as I ask. His leg rises from the water. As it does I see the damage the grenade has done. Bill can't feel his foot because it is gone. All that is left is bone and bleeding flesh halfway between his knee and where his ankle used to be.

Bill sees it too. "That ain't good is it, Trap? I'm in a world of trouble, I fear." Bill has gone as white as one of our sails. His eyes flutter. His breath comes in ragged gasps.

"Ye'll be right as rain," I tell him, though the wound is not good at all. We are in quite the predicament. The pair of us float between the bows of the ships, easily crushed if the ships move. If we cry out for help? We would be easy targets for a sharpshooter in the rigging. My stomach constricts into knots when I realize we may have another problem as well.

Some say sharks can smell blood in the water a mile away. They are a portent of death. Battle's coming soon enough, and the sharks are waiting around for a meal.

I look to Bill. He is barely conscious, from pain or blood loss, I can't tell. What I do know is that I have to do something or my friend will die in the water. I've already lost Tom and the rest of my mess; I will not let Bill suffer that same fate.

"Keep yer leg still." I try to keep the fear from my voice as

I picture the sleek grey shape of a shark, jaws open, swimming towards us. With great effort my friend raises his leg out from the water. I hold his wounded limb with one hand, blood still streaming out of the wound as I reach for my neck with the other. It's hard to untie my kerchief with just one hand but somehow I manage to release the knot.

"Hold tight while I stop the bleeding," I tell Bill as I tie the kerchief tightly above the wound.

"Good idea," he says through gritted teeth. Wounded or not Bill understands our situation. "I'd hate to survive the battle and end up bleeding to death or in a shark's belly as his supper."

Overhead, shot after shot rings out, as does the clashing sounds of sword on sword. I watch men swing on ropes or leap across the void from one ship to the other, shouting war cries, or screaming in pain as a ball or a blade sinks into soft flesh or bone.

"Hold onto me as I paddle," I whisper. "We need to get out of the water and away from the ships. A fallen spar, an errant shot, and we're done for."

We hold onto the wood, keeping our heads low, my feet kicking slowly. It's only when we are fifty yards away I stop to rest. As I do, the sound of shots and clashing steel suddenly stops. "Who's winning, do ye think?"

"I don't know," Bill says. The sun has completely vanished, the only light we see comes from the stars that twinkle overhead, the windows of the houses onshore, and from the fires that burn on board both frigates.

Then shouts erupt in the darkness. "Three cheers for *Cerberus*! Three cheers for King George!"

"Huzzah! Huzzah! Huzzah!" a chorus of sailors reply in one voice.

"Well," says Bill. "It seems we did. What do you think, Trap? Do we yell out for help — or do we not?"

"What do ye mean?" I'm exhausted, too slow by far to pick up his intimation.

"I think it's time we say goodbye to the Royal Navy, don't you? Swim to shore, take shelter in some nice Sicilian inn, then make our way back to England and get your sister. I told you an opportunity would present itself. I just didn't think it would come at the expense of my foot."

"Do ye think we can make it? To shore I mean? In yer condition?"

"I don't see why not."

"What about the cap'n? Will he come looking fer us?"

Bill laughs softly then gasps in pain. "Hardly. There are bits and pieces of sailors all over the decks and at the bottom of the sea. When they take rollcall Captain Whitby will assume we perished. Ain't no way anyone's going to come looking for us. What do you think? Make up your mind quickly before the sharks choose for us."

I grin so widely I fear my teeth will give us away as I start to paddle again, moving through the dark waters away from the ships towards the Sicilian coast. "Aye, an inn sounds nice to me as well. I reckon we've done our duty to King and country."

Chapter 29

ALTHOUGH BARELY 500 yards away, the slow swim to the shore is gruelling. The tide runs against us, the water choked with debris from the battle and the bodies of the dead. Despite putting on a brave face, Bill is grievously wounded and I must hold onto him as well as the spar as I kick my feet towards land.

I nearly cry with relief when I hear the waves slapping on the shore, and feel the rocky bottom beneath my bare feet. Bill drifts in and out of consciousness, unable to stand or even crawl. With my last remaining strength, I pull him to the beach and half-drag, half-carry him up a small sandy beach to what I hope is a spot beyond the tideline.

Behind us on the water, fires still burn, though they are smaller. Either Royal Navy sailors have extinguished the flames on *Incorruptible* or the ship has burned and sunk to the bottom of the bay. Either way I am too exhausted to care. I check the kerchief tied onto Bill's shattered leg to make sure the bleeding has stopped. Job done as best I can, I fall to the sand beside Bill and the world fades away.

* * *

. I awake the next day to the mewling of gulls and the heat of the sun on my face. Groaning, I open my eyes and peer into the sky. The sun is high above us. I realize with a shock that it is noon, or just after. I've slept the night and all of the morning away.

I look to the sea. *Incorruptible*, *Unicorn* and *Cerberus* are not to be seen, although I hear the voices of sailors, the sounds of hammers and saws on the wind.

It is then I realize that we have swum into a small bay, protected by a narrow headland that blocks the sight of the open Mediterranean. This is fortunate. If I can't see the ships they can't see us.

"Bill! How are ye?" I look to my friend beside me. He lies still, his eyes shut. At first there is no answer and I fear he's dead.

"Bill! Wake up!" I cry as I shake him by the shoulders.

"Easy, Trap," he says in a weak voice, his eyes fluttering

open. "I may feel like death but I'm still alive. I thought we were gonna find a nice inn? This doesn't look much like one to me."

"I need to check yer foot," I say, relieved beyond words my friend still lives and can make a joke.

Bill struggles to sit up on the sand. "I think you mean my stump. If you're looking to check my foot you'd best swim out to *Cerberus* to ask the sharks if they ate it for tea. If they did, tell 'em I hope they choke on a toenail."

"I'm glad ye haven't lost yer sense of humour," I say as I move towards his leg.

"I've lost enough for one day, don't you think, Trap? What does it look like? Tell me true."

"It isn't a pretty sight." Halfway between Bill's knee and where his foot used to be his leg bone is visible. The bone is jagged, a large patch of flesh dangling underneath it. His leg is covered with dried blood while fresh blood still leaks from the wound. The tourniquet I made from my kerchief has saved his life, no doubt.

"I need to clean it," I say. "Give me a minute."

We have no clothes. No shirts, no hats, no shoes, just our dirty breeches. That outfit is fine enough for sailors on the deck of a ship but less so for two men washed up onshore.

I walk down to the beach. The bay is littered with debris. There is wood, rope, an entire sail even, untouched save for the holes ripped into it by chainshot. I can't help wondering if I was the one who shot it.

There is also a body washed up, birds landing and taking off beside it. Whoever it was, French or English, the near-naked corpse is already bloating in the sun. The poor wretch's eyes are gone as well, eaten by crabs or birds or some other scavenger.

A long knife hangs in a leather scabbard on his belt. This is a most lucky thing. While I still wear a scabbard on my waist I have lost my own knife, either from the force of the explosion that knocked me off the ship or during the swim ashore.

I reach down to the man, nose wrinkling in distaste at the stench of death. His body is riddled with holes, one large enough for a crab to crawl in and take refuge. I take the knife from its scabbard, tuck it into my own then walk away. I have an important task to attend to, after all.

I cut a chunk of canvas from the sail then using it like a makeshift water skin, the sort I used in New Caledonia and along the river, I collect sea water then return to my friend.

"What did you see?" Bill asks. "Can you tell what happened?"

"I cannae see the ships from here. We're in a bay of sorts. I'll go fer a look later but fer now ye need me to tend to yer leg." Salt water is as good as anything at cleaning wounds, I learned at sea. Bill grunts in pain as the sea water washes over his leg, but he bears up well enough to let me do my work.

"Guid enough," I say. "Fer a few hours at least."

I carefully untie the kerchief, ready to knot it back up if a rush of blood pours from his leg. While some does, it is just a wee amount. This is good news. While my friend may yet die of infection or fever, at least he won't bleed to death.

Gently I wrap the canvas around his stump then tie it off with the kerchief.

"You sure you weren't a doctor instead of a fur trader in the wilds of Canada, Trap?"

"I've seen my share of cuts and scrapes and have tended more than a few in my travels, 'tis true." On my way across North America and down the river with Simon Fraser there were many injuries. Gagnier with the swivel gun that blew up when he fired it. Fraser's fall and injured leg when he narrowly missed a bite from a rattlesnake.

Though I am no doctor I did watch and learn a few things about healing from the voyageurs, the people of the river, as well as from the sailors. "If I had bear grease I could work miracles."

Bill is completely confused. "Bear grease? What on earth are you talking about, Trap?"

I smile. "Never ye mind. 'Tis a little trick I learned to heal feet ripped up by sharp rocks and cacti."

"I think I need more than bear grease to fix my foot."

"Aye, yer right about that. The best thing right now is rest and salt water. Let's find ye a more comfortable place to sit."

I help Bill up. He hops gingerly along as I wrap my arm around his waist and help him off the beach towards a spindly tree next to a rocky bluff.

I place Bill down, his back resting against the trunk of the tree. "How's that?" I ask.

"Not quite a king's throne but it will do."

"Guid. Now wait here. Get some sleep if ye can while I see if there's any fresh water to be found. I haven't done all this work saving yer life only to have ye die of thirst on me."

Chapter 30

I RETURN TO THE beach to cut another chunk of canvas from the sail, doing my best to ignore the body. I will search later to see if any other useful items have washed up, but I must find fresh water first.

There is a narrow footpath that follows the beach. Weeds grow along it, and I can tell that it is not used frequently. I look to the north. From the deck of the *Cerberus* I saw the twinkling of lights a mile or two from our present location.

A time may come when I need to follow the path towards the town, but today is not that day, not with the ships still anchored offshore. We can't afford to trust the people who live there not to turn us over to the Royal Navy.

I scan the coastline to the south. From my travels in the wilds I know that creeks and rivers often flow in draws and small valleys. Some three hundred yards down the coast I see such a thing. Canvas in hand I set off along the beach, walking carefully. I have no shoes after all, and though my feet are hardened by weeks of walking barefoot on the deck of the *Cerberus*, sharp rocks and spiny plants will still hurt.

As I clear the headland, *Cerberus* and the other ships come into view. I crouch down beside a twisted pine and watch the ships. I hear ship's carpenters busily swinging their hammers, repairing the damage done to both the *Cerberus* and the *Incorruptible*.

Both are still afloat, though even from some five hundred yards away I can see that the French frigate suffered significant damage. Her mainmast still stands, but the foremast is gone, its spars, sheets and sails shot away as well. No doubt remains that the piece of canvas I hold in my hand came from the *Incorruptible*.

The *Unicorn* escaped major damage during the battle and stands guard, her starboard guns point out to sea, ready to level a broadside on any enemy ship that approaches.

There is good reason for her to be wary. The other French frigate, *Revanche,* is still out in the Mediterranean somewhere, and would love to avenge the double insult we have given Napoleon's Navy. It will be bad enough that the *Incorruptible* lost the battle but to have her taken, repaired and turned into a Royal Navy ship will make the French furious.

Although I can't see them, I almost feel sorry for the French sailors. Those who survived the battle will now be locked inside their own hold, sweating in the heat and darkness. They are all destined, no doubt, for the same prison hulks that now hold the Russians we captured in the Baltic. Those old ships are death traps. Few will ever breathe free air again.

I walk furtively down the beach, keeping low. The odds of my being spotted by anyone on the ships are low, the chances of being recognized even lower, but I am free of the Royal Navy and plan on remaining so.

When I approach the draw I pause to listen. Through both my adventures in Canada and my time aboard *Cerberus*, my senses have been heightened. I focus on the sounds around me. I hear the gentle lull of voices and dull thud of hammers from the ships. I hear the wind and the waves breaking upon the beach. I hear the gentle twitter of birds. Then I hear the sound I was praying for.

A slight babbling rises on the wind. Water to be sure. I hurry forward, ignoring the pain in my feet as I step on sharp stones. There it is! A small stream at the bottom of the draw. It tumbles out of the Sicilian hills, ending here in a gentle trickle into the sea.

I put my head into the water, drinking deeply, feeling instantly better as the cool fresh water washes over me. Full for now, I turn the sailcloth into a makeshift water skin, just as I did when I collected sea water for Bill. I hurry back to my friend.

"It tastes better than the finest wine in all of Creation!" he says when he has drunk his fill as well. There is a little water left in the canvas, and though it isn't as waterproof as moose hide, and the water soaks through the sailcloth and drips onto the ground, it will hold it well enough for now. The creek is only a few minutes away and I can get as much as I need later.

"Do ye think ye can stomach a bit to eat?" I ask.

"You know where to find roast beef and carrots, Trap? Perhaps a nice apple pie?"

"Nae, though I'm sure I can scrounge up something." When I searched for water I noticed a grove of trees with unfamiliar green fruit on them. I walk back to the trees and take a closer look. They are thick, ancient-looking things, their branches heavy with the fruit, about the size of grapes but of a different shape. I pick a few and return to Bill.

"Do ye ken these fruits?" I ask. "Are they guid to eat?"

"Olives," Bill says weakly. "They're a bit salty but edible enough. At least we won't starve, not that I feel much like eating. Go ahead and have one."

I pop one of the small green fruits into my mouth. It is salty, on the greasy side as well, but I don't mind the taste. The hard pip in the middle comes as a bit of a surprise, however, as I bite down onto it.

"Sorry, Trap," Bill says. "I forgot all about that. Mind your teeth."

"Will ye be all right if I leave ye alone fer a bit?" The sun has started to dip on the horizon. It will be dark in a few hours and there are important things I need to do before that happens, including finding something a little more nourishing than olives.

"Go on. I'm fine." But Bill doesn't look fine to me. His words are slurred and he has broken out into a fierce sweat, his forehead and chest soaked with it.

"Let me look at yer leg." I unwrap the bandage I made from sailcloth and feel sick at what I see. The wound is red, and clear fluid drips from it. I feared this would happen. He suffered an awful injury and it is beginning to fester.

The flap of flesh and skin that hangs down from Bill's tattered leg looks dead and has begun to smell. It seems to me that it is the source of the infection that is taking hold of my friend. I know what I need to do, though I hate the thought of it.

"Hold on, Bill," I say, taking my knife. "Ye've got a bit here that's gone bad. I need to remove it. It may hurt a wee bit. Are ye ready?"

"Go on then," he says. "Get it over with, but do it quickly."

The knife I took from the dead sailor is sharp and will do the job, but do I have the stomach for what needs to be done? Gingerly I reach out my left hand and take the corrupted flesh. It feels slimy in my hand, and warm, full of poison.

"On three," I say.

Bill nods. "On three."

"One." Steeling myself, I move the knife towards his leg.

"Two," Bill says, taking up the count.

"Three." We speak at the same time the knife flashes through his flesh. A second later the piece of what used to be part of Bill's leg is in my hand, blood and pus flowing out of it.

Bill does not scream but his groan tells just how much it hurt him. "All done," I say, throwing the rotten flesh away. "Let me get some more water to clean it, then I'll patch ye up and ye'll be right as rain."

I hurry to the beach with my water skin, returning quickly to Bill. He is barely conscious now, and does little more than whimper as I wash his leg, then take a fresh strip of canvas sail and bandage him up again.

"How are ye bearing up?" I ask.

"I've felt better, Trap. Can't say I haven't." There is no smile in his shaking voice. He is desperately sick, I know. I have removed most of the rotten flesh but there is more remaining on his leg. Cutting it away could make him bleed to death. I have one option to treat Bill. One I care not to think about, but one I know I must do. But not quite yet.

"Rest, Bill. I'll be back in a bit." I shake the thought of that horrible treatment from my mind and return to the beach. The sail is the first thing I retrieve, cutting it free from the spar with my knife.

Again and again I make the trip between the shore and our little camp, bringing back as much canvas, rope and fragments of wooden spars as I can carry.

I look as well for something I know I will need later

tonight. I search through the broken wood for ten minutes until I see what I am looking for. A piece of a door or hatchway has washed up onshore along with the other flotsam. On it is a large iron hinge. It is exactly what I need.

I return to Bill, make another small bag from the sailcloth and hurry back to the sea. There are mussels, clams and small crabs in abundance on the rocks. I am no fisherman but I've eaten clams before with Simon Fraser on the river just before we reached the Pacific. They are not my favourite, but I am famished and need my strength.

"One more trip fer water then I'm in fer the night," I tell Bill before I walk to the stream. He says nothing, a weak grunt his only response.

I make Bill drink a bit, then tie off the canvas bag and hang it from a tree branch. As the sun sinks in the west and the stars emerge in the darkening sky, the temperature drops as well. The breeze from the ocean has a bite I had not felt in the heat of the day.

I look to my friend. Bill shivers, though from cold or fever I cannot tell. I take a chunk of the canvas I've cut and place it over him as a blanket. I wish I had the buffalo robe Louise made me, the one that kept Luc Lapointe and me alive on the shores of Lake Superior, but I left that behind in Montreal in the care of Mr. McGillivray. It will serve Bill no good there.

With what little light remains I gather twigs, dry branches and dead moss. I need to make a fire both for light and for heat. In the day the smoke would have given us away to the men back on board *Cerberus* and *Unicorn*, but at night and with the headland between us and the ships, I believe I can light a small one and not have the flame seen.

It is simple enough to make a fire. Luc Lapointe taught me that not long out of Lachine. Steel and flint are all a voyageur needs. I have steel enough with my knife and flint pebbles are everywhere on the beach. I gather some small dead twigs and make a small tipi with them. A few quick strikes of the side of the knife on the rock and I soon have a nice fire.

I feed it branches until it crackles merrily, then I throw in several pieces of broken spar. The wood has dried in the sun and soon catches, thanks in large part to the pitch that covers the wood. Pungent smoke fills my nose, making me cough until the breeze blows it away.

"Dinner time fer me, Bill," I say, getting the mussels and clams I'd collected earlier. Bill is slipping in and out of consciousness. Food may not be a priority for him, but I must eat.

I put the shellfish and crabs on a flat rock I'd put in the fire for just this reason. Within minutes they pop and steam, their shells splitting open. I eat a dozen. They taste more like leather and sand than anything else, but having something hot in my belly is a treat.

Bill moans and thrashes around. I look to my friend worriedly. He is covered in a sheen of sweat that glows in the firelight. Time to do the only thing I can to try and save his life.

I had placed the hinge in the fire not long after I made it. Now it glows red-hot, hot enough to cauterize his leg, to burn the damaged flesh away and hopefully the infection with it.

I walk over to Bill. "I need to treat yer leg. The poison's took hold and if I don't ye'll die. I have to burn it, Bill, do ye ken what I'm saying?"

Bill's eyes flutter open. "Do it," he breathes.

"Bite down on this, then." I place my leather knife scabbard in his mouth then tie it down, wrapping canvas strips around his head to hold the thing in place. The leather will keep him from biting his own tongue off or screaming too loudly.

I return to the fire. I wrap my hand with thick wet canvas, draw a breath and take the hinge from the flames. Even through the damp sailcloth I can feel the heat of the thing, glowing red and yellow in front of me.

I return to Bill. "On three?" I ask.

He nods then shuts his eyes.

I sit on top of Bill. I'll need my body weight to hold him down, to keep him as still as I can. Then I begin to count.

"One." I feel the heat of the metal creep through the cloth.

"Two." Sweat breaks out on my own forehead as I start to lower the hinge.

"Three."

As I count three I press the red-hot metal firmly into the wound. I don't know what is worse: the sickly sweet smell of cooking meat, the sound his flesh makes as it sizzles and pops, the thrashing of my friend underneath me or the muted howls of anguish that escape the canvas and leather in his lips.

I lift the metal then touch it down again on more dead flesh. Then again, then again until I am certain I have burned away the rot. Bill screams again then falls limp.

Suddenly my own hand feels as if it is on fire. I drop the metal and roll off Bill. I hurry to my feet and to the canvas water skin, sticking my burning hand into the cool water.

"Bill! Are ye alive?" I return to his side and place my head upon his chest. It is faint but his heart still beats, his chest rising and falling with every weak breath.

A great wave of exhaustion sweeps through me. I collapse again to the ground beside my unconscious friend. I have done everything I can to help him. I feel the cool ocean breeze blow across my body, bringing with it an old memory of my journey with Luc Lapointe to Fort William. We were far from civilization, entering a lake the size of the sea.

Old Lady Wind. La Vieille will sink us in a heartbeat if we anger her, so we give her gifts to keep her happy.

"Please, *La Vieille*," I pray before drifting into sleep. "When we get back to England I'll give ye whatever ye want if ye keep Bill alive."

Chapter 31

THE SUN HAS long climbed over the eastern horizon when I awake. The day is warm, the air full of the chirring of insects and the cry of seabirds.

"Bill?" There is no answer. I turn to my friend in a panic, certain he is dead. He lies still beside me, not saying a word. But then I hear him breathe, see him gently stir. The sweat that poured from Bill's body is gone, and though he is pale he looks better than he did yesterday.

The metal hinge lies cold on the sand beside Bill. His leg is a sight where I burned him, charred like a rabbit on a fire. The awful smell of charred flesh remains but there is no odour of rot.

I get to my feet and walk down to the beach with a sail-cloth water skin. My own hand is red and blistered from the hinge. I grimace as I put my hand into the sea. The salt stings mightily but the water is cooling nevertheless.

I look around the beach. More debris has washed up, although nothing useful by the looks of things. The body of the sailor has gone, though. Eaten by crabs or carried away by the tide, I don't know. Either way I am grateful for it. The sight of the dead man seemed a sinister omen for what may happen to Bill. I take it as a fortunate sign the body has gone.

I return to our camp with fresh sea water. I gently wash Bill's charred leg. Even unconscious, he flinches as the water runs over the wound, but he does not cry out.

I'm not that hungry but I force myself to eat a few of the green olives. I have some work to do today, and the food will do me good. After I finish the olives, I get to business.

My feet are my first concern. While the beach is sandy and the path to our little campsite is easy enough to walk, the rest of the area around us is hard-packed and stony. We won't stay here forever and I know what it is like to have my feet shredded by sharp rocks. Fortunately there is something I can do about it.

"I met a great chief of the Secwepemc People once," I say, working a chunk of sail with the knife. Bill is still asleep and I know he won't answer, but it makes me feel better talking while I go about my job.

"His name was Xlo'sem. His people showed us how to

make moccasins when our own boots had fallen to pieces. I'd prefer deerskin but sailcloth will have to do."

Xlo'sem would have laughed at my poor attempt at moccasin making. They are little more than canvas bags, lined with moss at the bottom, tied on with a strand of rope, but they are functional enough. Now I can walk at least without fear of cutting my feet.

"I'm no tailor but I ken how to make a shirt fer each of us as well." I work the knife again on the sailcloth carefully, minding the blisters on my palm.

The people of the river wore deerskin breeches and tunics. They were skilfully made, decorated with the most wonderful beads and patterns. What I create has none of their art but will serve us well enough.

I cut a square of sail large enough to fit me. I slice a hole in the middle of it for my head to slip through. I fold it in half, poke holes in the sides of the canvas then stitch the two halves together with lengths of hemp I've peeled from a piece of rope. I leave enough space for my arms then slide my crudely made shirt over my head. I make another one for Bill, hopeful he will need it soon enough.

Job done, I return to the stream to collect more fresh water. I creep to the headland to see if the ships are still anchored offshore. I hope they have sailed off, but *Unicorn, Cerberus* and the *Incorruptible*, now flying the Naval Jack, are still there.

Bill sleeps for a full day and night and half a day more until he finally opens his eyes. "Water," he gasps.

"As much as ye can take, Bill," I say, putting a damp piece of canvas to his lips. I squeeze the water into his mouth and he gulps thirstily before drifting back to sleep.

* * *

"I don't suppose you ever found that apple pie, Trap? I could do with a slice right now." The sound of Bill's voice wakes me instantly. It is late afternoon of the following day and I have been dozing in the sun in our little campsite.

"Bill!" My face breaks out into a wide smile. "I cannae believe it!"

Bill pulls himself up to rest against the trunk of a tree. He grimaces with the effort but manages nevertheless. "Awake and hungry, Trap. Please tell me you've managed to find something else to eat other than olives."

"Let me see to yer leg first." I unwrap the salt-soaked canvas bandage. The skin around his stump has scabbed something fierce. It is a nasty sight to behold, but there is no sign of infection, no red strips up his leg nor rotten flesh. Bill is very weak but he seems to be on the mend.

"Thank you, Trap," Bill tells me as he inspects the leg. "You saved my life."

I blush at the compliment. "A dinnae ken about that. How are ye feeling?"

"Strange to be honest," he says. "I can hardly remember much of anything since our first day here. After that it all gets muddy. There are flashes, images really, more like dreams than anything else." Bill shudders when sees the iron hinge in the sand. "That I do remember. How long have we been here?"

"Tonight will be our fifth night onshore."

"Gracious! Five days! I've been out of it that long?"

"Aye. Dead asleep fer the most part. There were times I wasn't sure ye were ever waking up."

"And in all that time you didn't find any apple pie? I don't know what you've been doing with your time!"

I can't help but grin. "Nae, there's no apple pie but I think I can find ye something to eat."

I walk down to the beach in our sheltered little cove to collect clams, but before I do I scramble over the headland. I start when, instead of the ships, I see naught but empty sea.

Incorruptible no doubt has sailed back to England with a skeleton crew and her prisoners, repaired enough to travel, a great prize for the Royal Navy. *Cerberus* and *Unicorn* on the other hand will have pulled anchor in search of *Revanche*. Capturing *Incorruptible* came at a terrible cost, but the job is only half done. Captains Whitby and Kerr, loyal to King and Empire, will scour the Mediterranean one bay at a time until they find the French.

I climb down to the beach to collect clams, feeling happier than I have in ages. My friend is alive and the ships have gone. Tomorrow I will try to find a way off Sicily, the first step in a journey that will take me back to England and, God willing, to Libby.

Chapter 32

"SO WHAT NOW?" I ask Bill.

"Well, Trap, I ain't up to much walking just yet, so it seems to me that our best option is to sail to friendlier shores. We came here to save Malta so perhaps Malta can repay the favour. The island's just a day's sail from here to the south. If we can get there and avoid the Royal Navy we should be able to find passage on a merchant ship back to England."

Bill tries to struggle to his feet, leaning heavily on the crutch I have made him from a branch cut from a small tree. The effort is too great and Bill gives it up, settling back down against the trunk of the tree with a grunt. "There's only one problem with the plan as I see it, though."

"Aye? And what would that be?" I ask.

"We don't have a boat, Trap. Hard to sail without one."

"Leave that to me," I tell Bill. "I'll return in a couple of hours."

I leave a puzzled Bill behind. From the deck of *Cerberus* we could see a collection of lights a mile or so to the north of our present location. That is where I need to be. As I walk up the narrow path towards the village, I run my fingers along the waist of my trousers.

When I first received my uniform they were white and crisp and new. Now? My trousers are soiled and stained with tar, blood, smoke and gunpowder. The fabric has worn thin, has torn in a dozen places, but my coins, half my wages for my time in the wilds of Canada, are still sewn into the lining.

I pause for a moment. I pull my knife from the leather scabbard. I can see Bill's tooth marks, where he bit down into the leather when I cauterized his leg. I cannot imagine the pain he felt, and I am grateful beyond measure he survived, that I didn't kill him.

I make a small slice in the waist of my trousers and push six silver coins through it. I keep the rest, a dozen or so, safely hidden. Coins in hand, I carry on towards the village.

There were no merchant ships at anchor off the village or tied up onshore. Our best bet on getting off the island is to either pay a fisherman to carry us to Malta or purchase a boat and sail there ourselves, although I don't know the heading we must follow.

I consider this problem and several others as I follow the path as it twists alongside the rocky coast. An hour's walk from our campsite I see the first sign of civilization. An old boathouse, dilapidated and abandoned, sits sagging on the shore.

No one is about so I carry on walking. More old buildings appear, as do several ancient boats. They are hauled up on the beach, flipped upside down with holes in their bleached wood bottoms. None of these will serve Bill and me.

A few minutes later I see a thin tendril of smoke rising into the air. A fireplace or campfire burns up ahead, no doubt, and it will be there where I find people. I steady my nerves before I press on.

Rounding a corner of the path I see a well-kept stone house, fifty yards or so up from the beach. The smoke I saw climbs from a small chimney on its roof. The beach here is narrow and stony. Sitting on a large rock a few feet from the shore and beside a fishing smack I see an old, gap-toothed fisherman with a grey beard and a flat cap on his head.

The man is fixing a fishing net, his focus on his work. "Hello," I say as I approach. He turns at the sound of my voice, dropping his net onto the pebbled beach.

"*Buongiorno,*" he replies, eyeing me suspiciously. I can't say I blame him. I must look a sight with my canvas moccasins and shirt. "*Sei un marinaio?*" the man asks. I stare blankly at him, not understanding. The man tries again.

"*Sei un marinaio?*" he repeats again, pointing at me, then

the sea. He salutes me and puts his hands in front of his eye as if he were holding something. Suddenly I understand. He is pretending to use a spyglass.

"Ah! Sailor! Yes. I am a sailor."

"*Inglese o francese?*" That much I understand.

English or French? I debate for a second, attempting to tell the Sicilian fisherman I am neither. That I am in fact a Highland Scot from Loch Tay, but I don't think this fisherman would care about that very much.

"English." I hope the reply is the one he is looking for, and that he isn't allied with Napoleon.

The man grins. "*Inglese. Bene.*" He steps forward to shake my hand.

"Do ye speak English?"

"*No. Non parlo inglese.*" He points out to sea. "*Grande lotta? Boom boom?*" He mimics the sound of cannon fire. It is easy to see he is asking me if I was part of the battle off the coast.

"Yes. Boom boom."

"*Cosa vuoi, Inglese?*" He points at me and shrugs his shoulders. I think I understand this as well. He is asking me what I am doing here, or something to that effect.

"I have a friend. He's hurt and we need a boat and somebody to sail us to away from here."

The fisherman holds up his hands, confusion on his face. "*Non capisco.*"

He doesn't understand. I spoke too fast and said too much.

I must be clear and simple. There are several tidy boats pulled up onshore. I walk over to one of them. She is lateen-rigged, maybe twenty feet long and solid looking. It is smaller than I would have hoped for, but with a bit of luck, sturdy enough to sail us off Sicily. "Boat. To Malta."

"*Ah! Barca! Barca a Malta!*"

"Yes. *Barca* to Malta." I point at him. "Would ye take us there?"

He understands that as well. "*Me? No.*"

"All right then." And producing one silver coin from my pocket, I ask, "Would ye be willing to sell me one of yer boats?" It is time to show him some money. If the fisherman isn't willing to take us, then we must find a way to sail to Malta ourselves.

The man holds out his hand. The meaning is clear; he wants to inspect the coin to see if its value matches that of his boat. I have no idea how much the silver coin is worth here; all I know is that it took a month of hard travel to earn it back in New Caledonia.

"*Una moneta? No.*" He gives me back the coin then holds up all five fingers on his right hand. "*Cinque.*"

"So ye want to barter, do ye?" I feel hope. The man is interested in selling, and thanks to my work with the North West Company I know a thing or two about negotiating. If truth be told, I would happily give him the five coins if I had no choice, but if there is an opportunity to save some money I will take it.

I pretend I'm not interested. "Nae, thank ye, Sir." I start to walk away when he counters.

"*Quattro.*" Four fingers now stand up on his hand. Bargaining has begun.

I counter him back. "Two," I say. Holding up two fingers.

"*Due?*" the man laughs as if I have said a funny joke, or that I have insulted his very family. "*No due. Quattro.*"

I respond with three fingers. "Three."

"*Tre?*"

"Aye. Three. Not a penny more."

The sailor looks as if he's contemplating the offer seriously. "*Quattro?*" he asks again, hopefully.

I shake my head, lifting my fingers again. "Three."

He smiles. "*Bene. Tre.*" We shake hands, then I hand over the coins.

"Which way is Malta?" I have the boat, now all I need is a heading. Bill said it was to the south, but that is a vague direction in a sea as large as the Mediterranean.

The fisherman doesn't seem to understand so I try again.

I turn to the sea, pointing my finger to the horizon. "Malta?" I ask again, moving my hand from left to right.

"*Si! Malta. Bene.*" On the ground beside the fisherman is a large leather bag. He reaches into it and removes a small wooden box. He flips open the lid and I see a small mariner's compass.

He points to a direction on the compass rose, one I understand easily enough. "*Centocinquantacinque gradi. Sud sud-est.*"

"155 degrees. South by southeast. Thank ye," I say. "How far?" More hand gestures and the man understands.

"*Ah. Si. Centinaio miglia.*" After several attempts I get what he is saying.

"One hundred miles. Thank ye, Sir." One hundred miles. That is a great distance to sail. Twenty hours or more in the small one-sail fishing boat I have bought. Over that distance it is far too easy to get lost. I need his compass.

"Would ye consider selling me yer compass?" I ask the man, my hand gestures explaining what I want, another silver coin appearing in my hand as well.

"*No! Impossibile!*" he replies, but there is a shrewd smile on his face as he speaks. Negotiations have begun again.

Chapter 33

"AHOY, BILL! Are ye ready to set sail or do ye like this place so much ye want to stay?"

Bill is asleep, resting against the trunk of a tree when I return, dozing in the warm Mediterranean sun. Six of my coins are gone. Three for the boat, the other three for the old sailor's compass, a basket of dried fish, olives and bread.

I talked the sailor into giving me some kegs of water and one of wine as well. With the wind at my back, two hours of gentle sailing was all it took to return to our small bay.

"Sail? What are you talking about, Trap?" Bill asks sleepily, rubbing his eyes as he wakes up.

"Let me help ye up and ye'll see what I mean. A dinnae ken

about ye, but I've spent enough time on Sicily fer my liking."

Bill hops on his good foot, his arm wrapped around my shoulders, as we make our way slowly to the beach. "Well I'll be," he says in astonishment, looking at our little boat pulled up onto the shore, full of food and drink. "How on earth did you manage this?"

"Trapping, canoeing, shooting, bartering: we learn all sorts of handy skills in the North West Company. It's a twenty-hour sail to Malta, maybe more depending on the wind. The tide is ebbing, so do ye want to get underway or would ye rather wait fer the next one?"

"Then help me in, Trap," says Bill. "I'm as tired of this island as you."

* * *

Two hours later the coast of Sicily has disappeared behind us. There are other sails on the water, small fishing vessels and merchant ships that come and go to unknown destinations. They pay us no heed as we bob along on the waves. A lateen-rigged fishing boat is a common enough sight in these waters after all.

"South by southeast, Trap. Right on course." I man the tiller and handle the sail from the stern while Bill rests in the bow, handling the compass. We sail through the evening, and into the night when the sky falls purple and the moon and twinkling stars replace the sun.

"Time for you to catch some winks, Trap," Bill yawns. "I'll take over the tiller till morning."

"Aye," I say gratefully as my friend moves himself aft towards the tiller to take my place. "I could do with a wee sleep, I reckon." I stretch out in the bow of the boat, falling into a deep, dreamless sleep to the rocking of the boat.

✳ ✳ ✳

"Good morning," says Bill when I awake. "The weather turned a bit while you were sleeping, as you can tell."

"It did at that," I say, looking into the sky. It is early morning, perhaps an hour past sunrise as near as I can reckon, but there is no sun to be seen at all.

A thick fog has rolled in around us. The wind has lessened, the sails hang slack. We hardly move at all. We are still on course but at our current rate of travel it will take days, not hours to reach Malta.

"Fog's called the *Solano*," Bill says. "She rolls across the Mediterranean this time of year. Normally you'll find it further west, off the Spanish coast, but it's not unheard of in these waters either."

"I can hardly see ye in the mist," I say. "How long has it been like this?"

"We sailed into it an hour or so ago," Bill tells me. "It's getting thicker by the minute."

We can't see more than ten feet in front of us. The compass still reads 155 degrees, south by southeast. We are utterly dependent on it as we sail blindly through the fog.

Suddenly my ears prick up. "Did ye hear that?" I ask Bill. In the mist every sound seems exaggerated. I hear the creaking of the boat, the flapping of the canvas in the sail and the sloshing of water in the small bilge. But I hear something else as well, something off into the distance, I'm certain of it.

"Hear what?" Bill had drifted back to sleep until I roused him.

"There's something out there, I'm sure there is."

We listen for what seems like ages. I hear nothing save the sounds of our own boat. "I swear I heard something," I say after a moment or so. "Maybe I imagined it. Perhaps the fog is playing tricks on me."

Then I hear it again. Bill does too. "A voice," he whispers. "Look sharp, Trap. We ain't alone out here."

Chapter 34

THE FAINT TINKLE of a bell echoes through the thickening fog. "A ship," Bill whispers. We hear the distant murmur of voices as well, the words, the very language indistinct and unrecognizable. "Fishing vessel? Cargo ship, maybe. What do you think, Trap?"

"A dinnae ken what to think. I just hope it sails past without seeing us." I'm not sure why, instinct perhaps, but I doubt the approaching ship is a merchant vessel.

"There it is again," hisses Bill. The bell, louder this time, as are the sounds of people speaking.

Our eyes are everywhere, scanning the water for any

movement, any sight of a ship. The fog is thicker now than ever, and we see nothing.

"Trap," says Bill. "There, off the starboard bow, is it my imagination or . . . damnation!" Bill exclaims suddenly. "Ship for sure! Whatever she may be that ain't no merchant vessel, that's for certain! She's heading right towards us!"

A large dark shape looms towards us. We hear voices, much clearer now though we still can't make out a word they are saying.

"She's a frigate at least, maybe even a first-rate ship of the line," I whisper back, my eyes pinned on the huge form emerging through the fog.

"What do we do?" Bill asks, panic creeping into his voice.

I understand his fear. If the ship is Royal Navy, we will be picked up and pressed back into service. If she is French? Napoleon's Navy will not look kindly on two British sailors.

"Hold onto the painter and go over the port side!" I command Bill. "Keep the boat between it and us. Maybe they haven't seen us yet. If they do, they may think we're an abandoned boat and leave us alone."

"Or they may sail right over us, crush us into a million pieces, or see us, haul us up onto their deck and shoot us for target practice," Bill says taking hold of the long rope tied up on our bow.

"Aye," I reply climbing quietly over the side, lowering myself into the cool water. "They may at that, so if ye have a better plan ye'd best share it now."

It seems that Bill does not have any other ideas. He slips quietly overboard and swims towards me. Together the two of us press ourselves against the port side of the boat, in the space below the curve of her thwarts.

A few seconds later the ship emerges from the fog. She is huge with a very familiar name written on her bow.

"*Revanche!*" It is the other French frigate, and no doubt she will have heard of the loss of the *Incorruptible*.

Revanche means "revenge" in French, I know. Her captain will be sailing the Mediterranean in search of *Cerberus* and *Unicorn*, looking to live up to her name.

Our faces are tucked against the side of the boat, with barely our lips and ears out of the water as the *Revanche* pulls up alongside.

Though I am not fluent I picked up a fair bit of French when I travelled with the voyageurs. I listen intently as the sailors on board talk. The water laps at my ears and their accents are strange, but I manage to pick up the occasional word.

"... *un bateau de pêche* ..."

"*Voyez-vous son équipage?*"

"*Capitaine? Que ferons-nous?*"

I realize they are asking what they should do with our small fishing boat. The *Revanche* looms high above us, the top of her masts disappearing into the fog. Our little fishing boat seems a minnow beside a shark.

Shark.

I curse myself for thinking that word. The Mediterranean crawls with them. Who's to say there isn't one of the razor-toothed fish swimming up underneath us right now, ready to make a breakfast of me? I shut my eyes and pray.

"*C'est seulement un bateau de pêche.*" I hear a voice say from the deck. *It's only a fishing boat.*

With that the *Revanche* turns slowly away, off to find bigger prey than our little rowboat. Breathless we watch from the water as she sails off into the fog and out of sight. I wait another minute then pull myself out of the water. "Give me yer hand, Bill," I say to my friend.

"Thanks, Trap," he says gratefully, taking my outstretched arm. Bill is still very weak from his injury and lacks the strength to climb into the boat himself.

"Well that was lucky," Bill gasps, lying down on the deck of our little fishing boat. "I thought we were gonners for sure."

I check our course with the compass, adjust our sails and take my place at the tiller. "So did I. Now let's hope the fog lifts and the wind picks up. Guidness knows what else is sailing in this damned fog!"

Chapter 35

AN HOUR LATER I get my wish. The fog burns off, the winds pick up and soon we are sailing briskly over the blue surface of the Mediterranean.

"There! On the horizon! Do you see it?" I strain my eyes to the horizon where ahead a light brown island comes into view.

"Malta?" I ask.

"Yes, if the heading your Sicilian friend gave you is right. If not? We're looking at Africa and are sailing towards the Barbary Coast and a life in the slave markets."

"Then let's hope that old fisherman was right." We have no choice but to press on, after all. The fish and bread I purchased in Sicily are all but gone, as is half of our water and wine. Whatever land it is ahead of us is where we now must sail.

* * *

By early evening we approach the twinkling lights of a large port. "Valetta," Bill tells me. "Malta's biggest town. It seems your fisherman was right after all."

Valetta. I've heard that name before, but I can't quite remember where, not that I have time to stew on it as we enter the harbour and tie up at the dock. "It's a little late in the day to go walking about strange streets, don't you think, Trap? Do you have coin enough left for a room and some supper?"

"Aye. A soft bed and a hot meal would do me fine as well." There are several small inns along the waterfront. We find one, get a room, and then eat. I'm exhausted after a long day on the water, and despite my excitement I drift off to sleep almost immediately.

The next morning, once we are up, we see Valetta for the first time in sunlight. "She's a pretty enough port," says Bill. "A man could make a good home here, I reckon. That is if one didn't have a very pressing reason to return to England."

"Aye, one could at that," I say. The town is crammed with white and yellow stone buildings that start right at the waterfront. "But fate has other plans fer me right now."

"So what's the plan then?" Bill asks. The inn cost little enough, but money will become an issue if we are forced to stay in Malta for any length of time. Half of my coins are gone and goodness knows how long the rest will last. Getting some more money is a priority.

"Finding a doctor to look at yer leg, selling our boat, buying some decent clothes and getting passage on a ship back home," I tell him. "In that order if ye are fine with it."

Bill is. We ask for help from a man who speaks English and he directs us to a doctor's surgery, three blocks off the waterfront.

"My name is Dr. Curmi, and that's quite the injury, young man," the doctor says when we enter his surgery. "A sailor's wound all right. Chainshot or a grenade judging by the damage. Whoever cauterized it saved your life, no doubt."

"That was my young physician friend here," says Bill. "Trap ain't much of a cook but he makes for a fine doctor."

"He does indeed." The compliment is welcome, but we have more important things to do. "What can ye do fer my friend?" I ask. "We can pay."

Doctor Curmi examines the wound carefully. "You're not going to want to hear this, I'm afraid, but I'll need to cut a bit more off your leg. The bones are jagged where the shot took your foot; I have to even it off, then fold a flap of skin and flesh underneath it so you can wear a peg or a wooden leg."

Bill looks ashen as he grits his teeth. "I was afraid you'd say that."

The doctor coughs politely. "You said something about your ability to pay, young man?"

I give the doctor one of my precious six remaining silver coins. "Will this do?"

"Enough for the procedure and a wooden leg afterwards if you like," he says. "Although you'll need to let it heal a month or so before you'll be ready for the leg."

"It will hurt like the blazes, won't it?" Bill says.

"I have some good news for you in that regard," the doctor says. "We Maltese have been at the crossroads of the Eastern and Western worlds for centuries, and have learned much from both. The Arabs on the African coast may have earned the reputation of pirates of late, but they have forgotten more about medicine, astronomy and math than the most learned Europeans have ever known."

He walks over to a large shelf and takes down a glass jar. "Inside is something Muslim doctors call the soporific sponge. It is just what it sounds like," the doctor says, as I look inside to see a sponge soaked in a dark liquid.

"You're not going to cut my leg with a sponge?" Bill jokes, somehow finding his sense of humour once more.

"No, my friend," says Doctor Curmi. "The sponge is imbued with a mixture of herbs and medicines. I am going to place the sponge under your nose. You will inhale the medicine, fall asleep almost instantly and feel nothing as I cut your leg."

Bill scoffs. "It sounds like a child's fairy tale to me. Go ahead then, Doctor. Show me."

The doctor shrugs. "If you are ready I see no point in

delaying the procedure. Take off your breeches, lie down on my table and we will begin."

"Bunch of rubbish," Bill says as he removes his soiled and ripped Royal Navy uniform.

The doctor puts a pillow under Bill's head and covers him with a crisp white sheet, all save his damaged leg. Then he wraps a piece of cloth around his own nose and mouth.

"Are you ready?" he asks, as he uncorks the glass jar and takes out the sponge with a pair of metal tongs.

"Have a go then," Bill says with a tone of utter disbelief.

"Breathe deeply," the doctor says as he places the sponge under Bill's nose. I catch a whiff. It is strong, medicinal and heavily perfumed. My eyes water and my head swims at the smell.

"Go on then," Bill says. "Put your magic potion to . . ." He doesn't finish the sentence. Instead Bill lies quiet and still, completely knocked out.

"Put this back on the shelf, would you?" Doctor Curmi asks me as he replaces the sponge and the cork in the jar. Then, the doctor removes a leather strap, linens, a wicked-looking knife, a saw and some needle and thread from a drawer under the table. He puts them beside Bill's leg then fills a bowl with clean water.

"This will take only five minutes," he says to me as he tourniquets Bill's leg just as I did a week or so ago. "Your friend won't feel a thing and he will be fine when he wakes up in an hour or two. Are you interested in watching? Helping, perhaps? You do seem to have a knack for medicine."

My stomach heaves at the thought of it. I've seen enough blood and bones for a lifetime. "Nae, thank ye very much," I tell him. "Ye're the doctor. Tend to my friend while I go and find him some new trousers."

Chapter 36

AFTER AN HOUR or so of haggling, I sell our little boat to a Maltese fisherman down at the dock. He pays me with a handful of brass and copper coins whose value I can only guess. I've sold the thing at a loss, no doubt, but I need money more than a boat.

Next I find a tailor shop. The man offers to make me clothes to my exact measurements, but I have neither the time nor the interest. Instead I purchase ready-made trousers and linen shirts for the both of us.

It costs fewer coins than I'd thought. Perhaps my bartering skills, honed in the North West Company, were better than I had imagined.

Next I go to a cobbler's shop. A few more coins and I buy

two pairs of good leather boots. I try at first to buy just one boot for Bill. The cobbler laughs when I explain why, but politely declines the offer. One foot or not, Bill is now the proud owner of a pair of new boots.

Business done, I return to Doctor Curmi's surgery. "How are ye faring?" I ask. Bill is groggy but awake on the doctor's table. His leg is neatly bandaged up. The doctor has cleaned up, and there is hardly a drop of blood to be seen anywhere.

"I can hardly feel my leg but my head hurts worse than the time I drank a triple share of grog," he says before drifting back asleep.

"The effect of the drugs," says Doctor Curmi. "The procedure went very well. I will keep him here for the night. You have a room in Valetta?" he asks.

"Aye, at the inn just off the harbour," I say. "A dinnae ken its name."

"The Minerva," says Doctor Curmi. "A decent place. I will have your friend delivered there tomorrow. Buy a bottle of spirits and wash the leg with it daily. If you do this and ensure he rests for at least two weeks, your friend will avoid both infection and a return visit to me."

"Thank ye, Sir. I am truly grateful fer yer help."

Doctor Curmi shakes my hand. "He's alive today because of you, my lad. All I did was tidy him up a little so he can wear a peg. Speaking of which, I will send along a crutch and a wooden leg as well. One of the effects of this ongoing war is that both are in great supply."

After this, I return to the Minerva and strike a bargain

with the landlord. In exchange for eight hours of my labour a day around the inn, he will provide room and board for Bill and me for as long as we stay. Promising to start my work first thing in the morning, I leave the inn for the waterfront. The sailors and dockhands down here will know all about the comings and goings of England-bound ships.

"We've not seen a British merchant ship for weeks," one says. "Too dangerous to sail these waters right now."

"Maybe shipping will increase soon with the capture of the *Incorruptible*," says another.

"Don't count on that," another says. "*Revanche* is still out there somewhere."

I say nothing about my own experiences with both French ships, thank the men and return to the inn for supper. Perhaps it is better there are no British ships right now, not with Bill unable to move. All I can do is wait, tend to my friend and hope.

Chapter 37

AS PROMISED, Bill is brought to the Minerva just after noon. He is carried on a stretcher by two strong men who take him up to our room and lay him gently on the bed.

I am in the yard, cleaning out the stable, when Bill arrives. I quickly put down my pitchfork and run up the stairs to see him.

"Quite the thing, ain't it?" Bill says looking at the wooden leg the men have brought with them. "Doc cut it to the right size but he says I won't be ready to wear it for a month, six weeks perhaps. Ain't it the damnedest thing you ever saw?"

"It is, indeed," I say. The wooden leg is just that: the lower half of a leg to replace the one Bill lost, complete with a wooden foot. Perhaps he can use the second boot after all. There is a leather harness that will fit over his stump and leather belts to tighten it in place.

"Doc says I'll walk with a limp, but when I put on breeches and a pair of shoes you'd never know it weren't real."

* * *

For the next three weeks while Bill recovers, I spend my days working for the landlord. Among my chores I dung out stables, repair the roof and walls, serve meals, and carry sides of salt pork and kegs of beer into the storeroom.

Each day after dinner and with my work done, I walk down to the waterfront to learn what news there may be of a ship. For the past twenty days I have seen nothing, but to my great surprise today I see a large triple-masted vessel tied up at dock. My heart leaps at the sight of the Red Ensign — she is British for sure. Not Royal Navy, but a merchant ship called the *Pelican*. I read the name with surprise. I know that name.

We could always use a good hand on board the Pelican. Name's Robert. I'm her mate. We carry goods, bound for Valetta. Are you sure, lad? The Mediterranean is a good bit warmer than England this time of year. It's worth it, to feel the heat of the sun on your face, even with Napoleon's fleet out there!

It comes back to me in a flash! That is where I heard of Valetta before — from the seaman in The Gun, just before I was taken by the press gang and given the King's Shilling.

I hurry down to the dockside and approach the ship. "Pardon me," I say to a sailor who disembarks down the gangway. "Is there a mate on board this ship called Robert? A hale, bluff bald-headed fellow?"

"Aye, what of it?" he asks suspiciously.

"I'm an old acquaintance of his," I respond. "I was hoping to have a word."

The sailor heads back up the gangway. "Wait right there," he says.

A few minutes later, *Pelican*'s mate appears. "Tim here said you were an old mate of mine," the man says eyeing me sideways, "but you don't look familiar to me."

"We met just the one time," I say. "In London at The Gun. Just before . . ."

The man's face breaks into a grin. ". . . before you got thumped on the head by the pressers! I remember you well enough, young man. I see you made it to Valetta after all!"

"Indeed I did," I say. "When are ye returning to England?"

"We'll be in Valetta for a week," he says, "unloading supplies for the Navy and picking up lace and cotton. About time we got back here, thank goodness for the Royal Navy. Captured one of them blasted French ships, and nobody's seen hide nor hair of the other one."

I have, I think to myself. Both of the frigates, and from closer than I wanted. "Robert," I say. "Ye asked then if I was interested in sailing with ye back in London. I declined yer kind offer at the time but I was hoping ye would take me up on it now."

Chapter 38

WHEN THE *PELICAN* sails from Valetta, Bill and I leave with her. I work in exchange for my passage and, as for Bill, though we speak little of it, the sailors figure out soon enough he lost his leg fighting the French and is treated as a hero for it.

"Best time aboard a ship I ever had, Trap," he tells me two days west of Malta. The wind is brisk and the sun warm as Bill lounges beside the mast. "No chores, decent food and no French gunner trying to blow me to Hades."

"I cannae disagree," I say. My tasks are light compared to those on board *Cerberus*, the weather is fair and there is no sign of French frigates or Barbary Corsairs.

Within the week we slip through the Pillars of Hercules

into the open Atlantic, head north past the coast of Portugal and across the mouth of the Bay of Biscay, a strong wind pushing us home.

Although it is summer, the farther north we sail the cooler it becomes, and off the coast of France I see rain for the first time in ages. "Almost home," Bill says that night at supper. "A day, two at most, and we'll see England."

Late the next day Bill is proven right. Ahead, at the edge of the horizon, a green land mass comes into view. "The Cornish Coast," Robert says. "I wager you two are pleased to see home again."

"I never thought I'd be so happy to see England," I tell him.

"We'll reach the Thames tomorrow afternoon," Robert adds. "We'll anchor off Southend, wait for the tide and sail with it up to London. Then you'll be home proper."

At dawn I slip from my hammock and climb onto the deck. The sun rises above the starboard side of the ship, casting rays of light onto large rock bluffs to the west. "The Cliffs of Dover," I say to myself. "Looks like I managed to lay eyes on them once again after all."

* * *

"Mrs. Elizabeth! Shall I take the baby for you?" a voice says. The *Pelican* returned to London not even a full day ago and already I'm at Plashet House, waiting to talk to Elizabeth

Fry. We said our goodbyes to Robert and the rest of the crew when the ship docked on the Isle of Dogs, then booked a room in a small tavern for Bill to rest. From there I went straight to Newham.

I stand outside the house's gates and look up to see a woman holding an infant in her arms, walking with another who appears to be a servant. "Are ye Elizabeth Fry?" I ask, startling the women as they approach me.

"Yes, and if you are a thief you are wasting your time," she says kindly but firmly, handing the baby to the nanny. "I have no money, but if you're hungry, wait here and I'll send Maggie back to the house for food."

"I'm not here to rob ye, Ma'am. I need yer help."

Fry's face narrows and she stares at me intently. "Do I know you, Sir? You have very familiar eyes."

"Nae, Ma'am, but I think ye ken my sister. Her name's Libby. Libby Scott. I believe ye met her in prison." I hope against hope that the old crippled sailor back in Liverpool told me the truth.

"Duncan Scott? Can it really be you?" I start at the mention of my name. "People in England think you're dead, but your sister told me you weren't. I have to say that a part of me didn't believe her until now."

"Ye tried to help Libby." The words fly quickly from my mouth. "She saved me, let me escape. It was my fault and she paid the price! Please! Tell me where she is! I heard she was to be sent to Australia!"

"Oh Duncan," Fry says tenderly. "Your sister didn't go to Australia."

"Where is she then? What's happened?" The thought of Libby dead hits me like a punch.

"Son," says Fry, a huge smile creasing her face, weeping what appear to be tears of joy. "Libby hoped you'd come back, prayed you'd find her, and it seems her prayers have been answered. You've just recently arrived from Canada, I take it?"

"After a short detour, yes," I say, not wanting to go into details. "Please, Mrs. Fry, I beg ye, I've waited long enough. I need to find my sister. Do ye ken where she is?"

"Yes I do, Duncan Scott," she says as my heart explodes with joy. "Libby is alive and well, and she has had a most remarkable experience that I will relate to you shortly. To see her, however, you will have to go on another journey, though this time you won't travel near as far."

Chapter 39

TWO DAYS ON the Royal Mail coach takes Bill and me to Bristol, in the west of England. Fry's family is in the cocoa business and Libby, I learned, among many other amazing things, has been living in Fry's Bristol house, in hiding with Fry's sister-in-law. Despite everything she has suffered, Libby is still wanted and would no doubt be jailed or transported if caught.

"Your sister is a remarkable woman if only half of what the Fry woman said is true," remarks Bill as the mail coach stops in the centre of Bristol.

"She is at that," I reply. Like my friend I can hardly believe the things Fry has told me about my sister, though the woman is a Quaker and would have no reason to lie.

"You're sure you know where we are going?" Bill asks as we climb down from the coach and make our way slowly up the street towards a large, twin-towered cathedral that dominates the skyline. Bill now wears his wooden leg but still uses a crutch to help him walk.

"Aye, Bill, I think I do. Mrs. Fry's directions were clear enough and Bristol is nothing like London. If I can navigate my way through that city I'm sure I can find my way around here."

Union Street. That is our destination and is easy enough to find. After several minutes of walking we reach the house I was told to find, a house with the name *Fry* written beside the door.

It is a tall, three-storey row home, made of the same stone that built the cathedral and almost every other building in the city, it seems like. I stand in front of the door, frozen, wanting my hand to rise up and take the knocker, but finding it can't.

"Go ahead, Trap," says Bill. "She's waited long enough. You both have."

My hand doesn't feel my own as I take the brass knocker and bang it onto the thick wooden door. There is no response from inside, no sound. I wait for what seems like forever, and am about to walk away when the latch turns and the door squeaks open on its hinges.

"Yes?" an older woman asks, appearing from inside the

house. She is dark and short, with raven hair tucked underneath a cap.

"Hello," I stammer. "I'm looking fer someone. A Scottish lass, Elizabeth Scott. Do ye ken her?"

She eyes me suspiciously. "There's no one here by that name," she says curtly.

I feel the wind knocked out of me at her words. "This is the Fry residence, is it not?" I say.

"What's it to you?" she demands.

"'Tis everything to me," I say. "I've been looking fer my sister fer years now, since she saved my life in Liverpool. Elizabeth — Libby Scott is her name. She's supposed to be here. Mrs. Fry said so herself, back in London. I need to see her."

The stony look on the woman's face fades, for just a second, at the mention of Elizabeth Fry. Then it reforms. "I'm sorry, but I've never heard of anyone named Libby Scott."

I stand in front of the door, head pounding. "Not here? Libby's not here? Why would Elizabeth Fry have told such a cruel lie to me, Bill?"

"Hold on a minute, Trap," says Bill from behind.

"Aye?" I reply, head reeling.

Bill steps up beside me. "Think about it. The Fry woman said your sister made quite a name for herself, is in hiding because of it, right?"

"Good day to you, sirs," says the woman, suddenly looking alarmed. She tries to shut the door but Bill steps into the threshold, preventing it from closing.

"You must leave now or I'll get the authorities!" she says. Bill ignores her. "This woman don't know us from Adam. Do you really think she'd admit to housing a fugitive to a couple of strangers?"

"Nae, I dinnae think she would." Bill's reasoning is making sense to me.

"That Fry woman told the truth about everything else, didn't she?" Bill asks. "Right down to the nameplate on the door. Why would she lie about Libby? Besides, she's nearly a saint she is, according to everyone in London. Lying ain't something a person like that would do, seems to me."

"I insist you leave at once!" The woman presses hard against the door, trying to dislodge Bill but he does not move.

"You've travelled across the world and back, Trap," Bill says. "What harm is there in taking a few more steps?"

Bill is right. After so much, after so long I will not give up now. "I'm sorry about this, Ma'am," I say, "but I cannae leave here without knowing fer sure."

With that I lean hard into the door, pushing it open, pushing the woman aside. "Libby! Libby Scott! Are ye here?" I cry as Bill and I sweep into the front room of the house, but there is no response.

"Libby Scott!" Bill takes up the shout as well. "I'm with your brother Duncan! Can you hear me?"

Still nothing. We go deeper into the house, past the parlour. "Leave this house immediately! This is shocking! I must protest!" the woman says, following us closely behind.

I enter the kitchen but it is empty. "Libby!" I cry. "Please, fer guidness sake if yer here, answer!"

At first there is no reply, the terrible feeling that Elizabeth Fry has played a cruel trick threatens to overwhelm me. Then I hear the sound of a door creaking open.

"Who did ye say ye were looking fer?" comes a voice behind me. I spin on my heels to see a young woman emerge from out of a pantry. She has deep blue eyes and hair the colour of summer corn. I don't reply, can't speak at all. I just stand there, staring.

"Good gracious, Trap," says Bill softly.

"I thought I told you to stay hidden," says the older woman crossly. The girl ignores them both.

"Do I ken ye, stranger?" she asks, peering intently at me. Her eyes start to water, and her hands shake when she realizes that I am no stranger to her, no stranger at all.

"Duncan?" Her voice is scarcely above a whisper. "Can it really be you?"

"Aye, Libby," I say as I take my sister into my arms, my journey of more than ten thousand miles finally complete. "It most certainly is."

"I CANNOT TELL YOU how sorry I am, Duncan," says Elizabeth Fry. It is a warm, late-September day. Autumn asters and crocus bloom purple and red in the walled back garden of the Fry house in Bristol as Libby, Bill, Elizabeth Fry and I drink tea.

Mrs. Fry arrived just the other day, to the delight of us all. "I had to leave London and come to our Bristol house myself to make sure all was in order," she explained. "I was so excited to see Duncan that I completely forgot to write him a letter of introduction. You were lucky to make your way past Mrs. Cavanaugh. She is very fond of Libby and quite protective."

"You were at that, young man," says Mrs. Cavanaugh, pouring fresh tea. Mrs. Cavanaugh, it turns out, is the Frys' housekeeper, a formidable Irish woman who'd done her best to keep Bill and me out of the house when we first arrived.

"Never mind all that," I say. "We're together now and safe at last."

"Together, perhaps, but not quite safe," Mrs. Fry reminds us. "Libby cannot be safe as long as she is in England. After all, she put her life at risk, and some corrupt rich and powerful men were brought to justice because of her. These are men with long memories and even longer reaches."

"Aye," Libby says. "'Tis a shame. I quite like Bristol, but I ken I cannae stay here."

"It is to that end I came," says Mrs. Fry. "Apart from making sure you found each other, of course." She reaches into a small leather satchel she has with her, and removes a leather pouch.

"This came for you just after Duncan left London," she explains.

"What is it?" Libby seems confused that anything should have come for her, let alone a mysterious bag.

"Payment for what you did," Mrs. Fry explains. "Your story sold a great many papers. I ensured that you would get a percentage of that for your great bravery in Newgate."

Mrs. Fry hands Libby the pouch. My sister gasps when she looks inside, as do I when she shows the contents to the rest of us. "'Tis a fortune!" I exclaim, staring shocked at the pile of gold and silver coins.

"Not quite a fortune and certainly less than she deserves for what she did, but enough to allow a brother and sister I know to get out of England and start a brand new life wherever they may fancy."

Libby holds the bag of coins tight to her chest. "So where shall we go, Duncan? Scotland? Malta? Ye said it was nice there."

After my parents' death, Scotland no longer holds any appeal, and while the port of Valetta was warm and friendly, I know that life holds more for us than a small city on a small island in the Mediterranean can provide.

"I think I ken a place." My mind is suddenly back on the *Sylph*, looking at the tidy strips of farmland that ran up from the banks of the St. Lawrence. "Perhaps it's time we finally sailed across the Atlantic together, Libby."

The money Libby has earned, along with my few remaining coins are more than enough to provide us with a grand life in Canada.

She beams at the suggestion. "Montreal?" she says. "Though I'm not certain I want to travel as far west as ye went."

"Aye, Montreal or near abouts is fine fer me," I say. Of course Bill and I have heard Libby's tale since arriving in Bristol, just as she has heard mine. She was fascinated with the stories of the voyageurs and my adventures in New Caledonia with Simon Fraser and the people of the river. Besides, farmland or not, I know I have a job waiting for me at the North West Company headquarters.

Once a Nor'Wester always a Nor'Wester.

Mr. McGillivray himself said that to me, and the head of the North West Company is a man of his word. That I know from personal experience.

Libby looks at Bill. "There's money enough fer three to travel," she says.

"I couldn't impose," Bill replies.

"Impose? Don't be ridiculous, Bill! Ye saved my brother's life on the *Cerberus*! It's the least I could do."

Actually 'twas I who saved his life, I think to myself but decide not to spoil the moment.

"In that case I say yes!" Bill laughs.

"So what do we do now, Duncan?" asks Libby. "Yer the world traveller, after all."

Before I can say anything, Mrs. Fry speaks up. "Somehow I had a feeling you'd consider going back to Montreal," she says.

"As you know my husband's family are chocolate merchants. They sell their wares across Europe and across the Atlantic to Canada and the United States. It just so happens we have a rather large delivery of chocolate scheduled to sail next week on the *Walrus* from Bristol to Quebec City. The captain is a friend of my family. He said there's room enough on board for two."

Mrs. Fry grins at Bill. "Though I'm certain he can squeeze in another."

"Elizabeth!" Libby hugs the woman at the news.

I can't help but hug Elizabeth Fry myself. "So, Libby, you

ask, 'what do we do now'? I suggest we pack what few things we have and then use a few of yer coins to get some guid winter coats. Believe me, it gets colder in Montreal than ye can possibly imagine!"

ABOUT THE AUTHOR

David Starr is a prize-winning author of five previous books. In *The Nor'Wester*, he told Duncan's story of fleeing Scotland to Canada, where he joins Simon Fraser on his epic 1808 voyage by canoe down the Fraser. *Bombs to Books* chronicles the stories of refugee children and their families coming to B.C. *Golden Goal* and *Golden Game* are young adult soccer-themed books for reluctant readers. *The Insider's Guide to K–12 Education in B.C.* is a resource guide for parents about the B.C. school system. David grew up in Fort St. James in northern British Columbia, and he now lives in Greater Vancouver with his wife, four children and a dog named Buster. He is one of the UBC Faculty of Education's Top 100 Graduates and a school administrator in Metro Vancouver. For further information and readings availability, visit www.davidstarr.org.

MARQUIS

Québec, Canada